ENRAPTURED REGENCY ROMANCE

CHARITY MCCOLL

PUREREAD.COM

CONTENTS

FOR THE LOVE OF A LORD

TAMING THE LADY

TO DELIGHT A DUKE

FOR THE LOVE OF A LORD

THE STORY OF LILLIAN CRAIG AND LORD ERROL CAMPBELL

1
A TERRIBLE TRAGEDY

What Lillian would remember for a long time, was first the smell of smoke that had bothered her as she was putting her charges to bed, and then the heat radiating from the stone walls. The Worthington Manor was the pride of Sleeper's Haven Village in Exeter County, the home of their own baron. The presence of their own noble man gave the villagers some form of security and pride. Lord Brian Worthington usually opened his home one weekend a month, for the general public to view it and have picnics on the beautifully manicured lawns. This made all the village inhabitants feel like they were a part of the family.

There'd been an open house that afternoon and the twins were exhausted from running all over the place. Lilly had only been in the Worthington household for a week but she felt as though she'd been working there forever. Henry and Stephen were boisterous five-year-olds who seemed to have endless energy and had kept her on her feet the whole day. Lady Caroline was a good guide and spent most of the day was explaining the history of the family and the manor, which had been renovated and added on to for decades. It was an old building but the baron was quickly turning it into a modern stately home.

By the time she had bathed the boys and fed them, they were already half asleep and she put them to bed, kissing their foreheads. Tonight at least, they didn't demand that she tell them a story. It was while she was getting ready for bed that she thought she smelled smoke, and when she reached above the fireplace in her bedroom, felt the warmth of the walls. The baron was working on built in heating to prevent lighting of fires in the rooms because of the smoke and also it was the modern way to go. Lilly thought it was odd that the walls were hot since it wasn't winter. Her last posting had been with a family who had built one of the most modern homes with all manner of new gadgets and they'd also had built in heating. Lilly tried to remember whether the rooms would be heated in summer but soon ignored everything but her bed, on which she flopped and was soon fast asleep.

Sometime in the night, Lilly woke up to screams and at first she thought she was dreaming. Then she saw torches outsides and what seemed to be a huge bonfire on the other side of the manor. It was the wing where Lord and Lady Worthington had their rooms, and her first thought was for the safety of the boys. Henry and Stephen were still asleep and she tried to shake them awake, but they were too groggy. Their rooms were unnaturally warm and she knew there was trouble.

"Help!" She screamed at the top of her voice. "Please help me," she carried Henry and ran down the stairs, just as someone broke through the front door. She didn't even wait to see who it was, but handed the still sleeping child over, then dashed back upstairs for Stephen. By the time they were clear of the house, it suddenly hit her that she hadn't seen either of her employers.

"Where are my lord and lady?" She grabbed one of the other servants' arm, but the man just shrugged her off, hurrying away. No one seemed to have seen Lilly's employers and someone pushed her backward, causing her to nearly let go of Henry's hand. She soon realized that she had to get the children to safety, even as the fire burned on furiously, the flames devouring everything in their path.

"Miss Craig," someone called out to her and she turned to see who it was. The roaring flames gave enough light for her to recognize Reverend Thomas Wharton, the local vicar. "What happened?"

Lilly could only shake her head, hands firmly holding on to the two little boys who were now sobbing. "I don't know," she said finally.

"Where is Lord Worthington, have you seen him and the baroness?"

"No, reverend, it's just the boys and me."

And it was only the two of them who survived the horrendous fire. Being a Saturday, most of the servants had gone to the village to either attend to family matters or else join in the local barn dance. It was only Lilly who'd been home apart from her employers and the little boys. The baron and baroness perished in the inferno for no one could reach them in time. Hours later as she was seated in the temporary safety of the vicarage, Lilly was left staring at her two charges, who were once again sleeping like little babies, unaware that their lives had changed forever.

"Darling, what do you think about this one?" Lady Abigail Wentworth held up a blue muslin cloth against her cheek. "Will it do for my going away dress?"

"Yes, my love, it most certainly will," Lord Errol Campbell had a fixed smile on his face and the muscles were straining. His face felt like it was carved in wax and he wondered how much longer he was going to be subjected to this torture, shopping for his bride's trousseau. Abby didn't understand that the last thing any man wanted to do was to be shopping with his soon-to-be bride.

"You look bored," she dropped the blue cloth and picked up another one which was peach in colour. "What about this one?" When Errol didn't immediately respond, she turned to him, pouting and making her lower lip tremble. It always got to him and he sighed inwardly as he pulled her into his arms. "I'm sorry for dragging you into all this," she said in a childlike voice and he wanted to grit his teeth. Abby was twenty-two years old but liked to behave like a two-year-old, especially when she wasn't getting her own way.

"I'm just tired as I was with a few of my tenants for much of the morning, sorting their various problems out. I'm quite exhausted but if you'd like to finish your shopping, we can return home."

"I won't be but a moment," now that she'd been allowed to continue shopping, Abby's face lit up again. It was nearly another three hours before Abby finally called it a day, and all because she wanted to take some hot chocolate at the roadside cafe just across the street from the milliner's shop where she'd been getting some hats.

Errol was sure that Abby wanted to sit outside just so everyone passing by could see the various hat boxes and other packages that she had. Abby was one of those women who loved to show off to everyone who was interested. A true London socialite, Abby never missed the chance to be seen, while Errol was the exact opposite. He preferred a quiet life but with his upcoming marriage, knew that it would be impossible.

Well, he thought, he'd made his bed and had to lie on it, for the sake of his estate. His gambler of a father had ruined the estate and his only recourse was to marry a woman who would come with a huge dowry, if he wanted to save himself from shame. Hence, Lady Abigail Wentworth, whose father though only a baron, was a very wealthy man. The dowry he'd offered had made Errol decide that he could put up with his spoilt and self-centered fiancée, even though sometimes he longed that the union would have been based on love.

Errol knew for a fact that Abby didn't love him, but he was handsome and according to him, he often felt like one of the items that she liked to collect and show off to people. That was the reason she always insisted on him accompanying her wherever her whims took her. He always told himself that it was a small price to pay for the restoration of his family estate, but it was just a matter of time before he couldn't take it anymore.

"Patience," he told himself, taking a deep breath as he opened the door to his bedroom later that evening. He deliberately kept it dark and the drapes were drawn all the time, just to match his mood these days. He needed the money but he also needed his sanity and wondered how long he was going to continue pretending to be the happily engaged groom-to-be.

2

CHANGE OF PLANS

y Lord Duke,

"**M** *Felicitations from the Vicarage of Sleepers' Haven in Exeter County. My name is Reverend Thomas Wharton and I am in charge of this particular vicarage.*

Seven days ago, there was a tragic fire in the village and it took the lives of Lord and Lady Worthington, our local baron and his lady. You may be wondering what all this has got to do with you, but Lady Caroline Worthington nee Sanders is probably familiar to you.

I have in my possession what I would call a letter with a special request from Lady Carol. This makes me wonder if my lady had a premonition that something would happen to her and was preparing for her children's future. My lord and lady had twin boys, Henry and Stephen and right now these poor boys are homeless. They're in the care of their governess, Miss Lillian

Craig who has been kind enough to stay on, even though she'd only been working for the family for one week prior to the tragedy.

To get to the point, Lady Carol indicated that should anything ever happen to her and she wasn't able to bring her sons up, that I should contact you. She named you as the boys' legal guardian, and that's the reason I have written to you. The vicarage can only offer a temporary home to these children and as their legal and sole guardian, you need to come to Exeter and take over responsibility for them.

Please get in touch with me as soon as possible, and I will be able to facilitate everything so these poor orphans can have a stable home again. They've lost everything, the poor lambs and more than ever, they need you, your grace.

In the Lord's service,

Rev. Thomas Wharton."

Errol read the letter three more times before it dawned on him that he was now responsible for two boys, whose ages he didn't even know. The vicar hadn't mentioned that in his letter.

Why had Caroline Sanders named him as the legal and sole guardian of her sons, and yet the only connection between them was his late brother, Alfred? From what he could recall, Alfred, who was set to be next in line as the duke after their father, and Lady Carol Sanders the only daughter of a baron had once been engaged. Carol's parents were dead and she was brought up by an elderly aunt who had passed away just a few days after she got engaged to Alfred. The two had been so deeply in love that for twenty-year-old Errol, it was sickening to watch them moon and fawn all over each other.

Then suddenly, the engagement was over and within days Carol got married to a man much older than her. It broke Alfred completely and he turned to drinking heavily. He stopped caring about his appearance and the estate and this worried his family. One evening as he was returning home from the local village pub, he stumbled into the path of an oncoming carriage that was going full speed. He was tossed aside, his head hit the pavement and he broke his neck. His body was found early the next morning by the village constable who was on his way to the small precinct where he conducted his law keeping matters.

Errol swore never to forgive Carol for his brother's death and he'd all but forgotten about her. But that was until the letter came to Dorchester. It was just by sheer luck that he'd come down to check on his few remaining tenants when a messenger delivered the letter. These days he usually spent most of his time in London as he prepared for his forthcoming nuptials at the insistence of his betrothed.

What would make a woman he hadn't seen in six years appoint him to bring her children up after her death? Was this her way of getting back at his family, but what had they done to her? She was the one who suddenly announced that her engagement to Alfred was over and left him to get married to another man. Or probably, Carol thought the Duke of Dorchester's family still had money like they did in days past.

He chuckled softly to himself, "Poor Carol, what my few remaining tenants bring in is hardly enough to feed this household, let alone taking care of the needs of two growing boys." Dorchester Estate was in a mess and the last thing he wanted was to get involved in someone else's problems. Then, there was Abigail to consider. From what he knew about her, she wasn't one who would agree to his taking on children no matter their ages. She loved being the centre of attention and would never consent to sharing his affections with anyone else.

Errol had no experience with children and in the absence of family he hadn't even had the luxury or bane of dealing with nephews or nieces. Perhaps if Alfred had lived, by now he might have been an uncle. The thought of two children coming into his life was quite bewildering and the sudden responsibility thrust upon him was frightening.

Knowing the boys' ages might have helped but even as he thought that, knew that it wasn't entirely true. The closest he'd ever come to interacting with children was when he had to give instructions to his two stable boys who were about sixteen. What did one do with little children, he wondered, for he guessed Carol's sons to be anywhere between one to five years old. How was he expected to effectively communicate with children that young so as to understand their needs?

Then he laughed in self derision. He was getting way ahead of himself because he didn't think he was up to traveling hundreds of miles to a village somewhere in Exeter to take on a responsibility that he had no idea why it had been given to him.

"Miss Craig, I know that you've only been governess to Henry and Stephen for a few weeks, but would you consider waiting until their guardian comes before leaving?"

Lillian turned her sorrowful blue eyes to the vicar. "I wish I could do that, but I received an invitation for a new posting in London, and according to Lady Imogene, I need to report within a few days or the post goes to someone else. It's a good job and the pay is also attractive. They also mentioned that the family travels a lot and I would love to see the world someday."

"I understand, but find it in your heart to wait just a little bit. Once you've handed the boys over to their guardian, Lord Errol Campbell from Dorchester, you can then leave. See how these little ones are so attached to you," he pointed at Henry and Stephen who'd refused to leave her side even for a moment. The only time Lilly got any rest was when they were asleep, but even then she had to be alert for her two charges had started experiencing nightmares.

It was two weeks now since their parents had perished in the fire and there was barely anything to be buried. The boys had wept as she tried to explain to them that their father and mother were no more and were now resting in heaven. Lilly felt their pain and confusion and wished she could do something for them, but she also had a future to consider. Besides, the boys' guardian would be coming to take them away soon, though she wondered when since according to Reverend Wharton, he hadn't yet responded to the letter sent.

What if the guardian was dead, or worse, didn't want the little boys? What if he was an elderly man who could barely take care of himself, let alone two very active little boys? What would happen to them? Already, she'd heard one of the women in church talking about putting the children into a foundling home and it broke her heart just thinking about it. They had no living relatives, at least none that had been traced yet. Who would pay her wages now?

"I want Mama," Henry muttered, his voice shaking and eyes filling up with tears. On seeing his brother's sorrow, Stephen put his left thumb into his mouth and started sucking it. Hitherto, Lilly hadn't seen such behaviour from the boy and it caused her concern. The little boys were grieving and much as the vicar and herself had told them about heaven and seeing their parents one day, they still didn't fully comprehend the concept of death. "Miss Lilly, I want Mama."

"Oh my love," she kissed his forehead. "You have Stephen and me," she pulled both boys close. "We'll be alright," she said as much for herself as for the boys. She really had no idea what she was going to do about the two of them. Her face was creased in concern above the boy's heads and she bit her bottom lip anxiously.

3
OFF TO EXETER

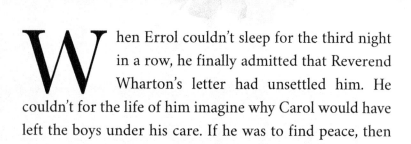

When Errol couldn't sleep for the third night in a row, he finally admitted that Reverend Wharton's letter had unsettled him. He couldn't for the life of him imagine why Carol would have left the boys under his care. If he was to find peace, then he was going to have to go to Sleepers' Haven in Exeter in order to appease his mind.

One person wasn't too happy with his decision, however. "Those children aren't your responsibility," Abigail screamed at him. "Didn't you tell me that your brother is dead because of that woman? That she broke off their engagement and caused him to begin drinking heavily? And now you're thinking about going off to the end of the world..."

"It's Sleepers' Haven," Errol found himself interrupting his already angry fiancée and thought she would explode.

"Exactly! Where is that village located?'

"In Exeter."

Abigail glared at Errol like she would have liked to say something more and he knew he had to do all he could to appease and bring her to his side. A lot was at stake and he didn't want to lose her, not at this time in his life. Walking over to her, he took both her hands in his. "My love, you don't have to worry about anything. It's you that I'm going to marry and will spend the rest of my life with."

"You don't have to go to Exeter, why don't you just send money so those brats can be put in an orphanage? I'm sure the church runs one, and then they will cease to be your responsibility. Every year, we will be sure to send our donation to the orphanage for their upkeep."

"Please understand, at least let me just go and find out why Carol chose to make me their guardian. There must be something more to this than we're seeing."

"I don't agree. That woman ruined your brother's life and now she wants to ruin our lives too," Abby let the tears run down her cheeks. "Don't you see? She never liked your family and now that she heard we were engaged, she deliberately made you the children's guardian. She has ruined me," Abby put the back of her hand on her forehead and dramatically sank into one of the cushioned seats. "My life is ruined."

Errol wanted to roll his eyes at the theatrics but sighed instead. "Should I decide to take on this responsibility, Henry and Stephen's presence in this household won't interfere with our lives. Besides, they'll always be with their governess and maids so we don't have to see them. But since I was named their guardian, at least let me go down to Exeter and see what needs to be done. If I have to bring them to Dorchester, we will both decide what to do."

It was a very reluctant Abigail who allowed Errol to get into his coach and leave for Exeter. He'd expected some resistance from her, but not to this extent. How could he just relegate the children to an orphanage without finding out why their mother thought he was the best person to bring them up?

It was a puzzle that he wasn't able to solve even by the time his footman drove the weary horses into the best inn in the village. Horseshoe Inn was owned by a harassed looking man and his equally agitated wife, but they gave him what they termed their best room.

"Oscar, we'll just have to make do with these shabby quarters, but take care that nobody makes away with our horses."

"Yes, your grace."

Lillian was giving the boys their simple breakfast of fresh bread and warm milk, when she heard a carriage drawing up to the front door of the vicarage. Reverend Thomas stood up and looked out through the window, then turned to her with a huge smile on his face. "That must be his lordship."

"His lordship?"

"The boys' guardian. The one their mother appointed."

"How would you know? Quite a number of carriages drive up to the vicarage from time to time."

"Not one emblazoned with what is obviously a family crest. Wait here."

When Rev. Thomas walked into the small dining room with a tall and distinguished man in his mid to late twenties, Lilly gasped audibly. She'd imagined an elderly looking man when the vicar mentioned that the visitor was a nobleman. This gentleman was handsome, but more than that, Henry and Stephen would look exactly like him in twenty years' time down to the colour of their eyes and dark hair! And all blood had drained from his face and for a moment she worried that he was about to swoon.

Errol took a step into the dining room and stopped abruptly, the shock on his face evident. It was like looking at a double version of himself some years ago.

Reverend Thomas had a thoughtful look on his face, and then gave a small nod. "It's like looking in a mirror nearly twenty five years ago, isn't it?" He commented in a soft voice.

The boys just gave the visitor a cursory glance before returning to their breakfast.

"This is Miss Lillian Craig, the boys' governess. This is Stephen and Henry."

Errol was still too shocked to speak.

"Your grace, please come with me." Once they were in the vicar's small office, Errol was handed a glass of brandy. He took a sip, grimaced at the taste and put it aside. Taking a deep breath, he turned to his host. "What is going on, Reverend?"

"You tell me."

"I don't even have to ask why Carol named me the boys' guardian."

"She confessed to me a few months ago, around the same time when she gave me the letter naming you as guardian. I wanted to know why, when her husband was still alive and she told me an interesting story about a young man named Alfred."

"My older brother."

"Apparently, when Miss Caroline found out that she was pregnant, she mentioned it to her beloved. They'd been in love and were going to get married, so she expected that Alfred would own up to the responsibility and push the wedding date forward. Unfortunately, things didn't turn out the way she hoped, so she had to find a way out."

"But Alfred never told me any of this."

"Alfred told Lady Caroline that he wasn't ready to be a father or something like that, and afraid to be made the laughing stock of Dorchester and London, the young woman accepted the suit of an old family friend, Lord Brian Worthington." The vicar shrugged. "They had a happy marriage and Lord Worthington loved the boys as if they were his own. At the time, I thought they were his children but when Carol told me her story, I finally understood."

"It's so amazing how much they look like my brother."

Reverend Thomas chuckled. "You should take a closer look into the mirror, your grace. You and your brother must have really looked alike."

Errol smiled sadly, "We were often mistaken for twins, regardless of the fact that Alfred was two years older than me." He sighed, tapping his fingers on the table. "I have to take the boys back to Dorchester with me, but I don't know who will look after them."

"Why not offer Miss Lillian the post? The little ones are quite used to her and she's good with them. She'd only been with the family for one week when the tragedy happened, and in all this time she hasn't received any wages, but she hasn't run away. You should be aware that one or two other wealthy families have tried to get her to go and work for them but she refused to abandon the two boys. She said she would wait to hand them over to you before moving on to her next posting."

"Is that the young lady seated in the dining room with the boys?" At the vicar's nod, Errol groaned inwardly. It wasn't that he doubted Lillian Craig's credentials and ability to take care of the boys, it was just that he had a very jealous fiancée. He was sure Abby wouldn't welcome the presence of another woman in his household, regardless of the fact that she was the boys' governess.

"Is there a problem, your grace?"

"I want the boys, they're my blood. It's what Alfred would have wanted, and since this is so, the older twin is actually the one who should be the duke, since I only got to be that because of my brother's untimely death."

"Well, no one is stopping you from taking them."

"It's the governess. Isn't she a little too young?"

"Miss Craig may look young, but she's very competent. Or is there another reason why you think she might not be the best person to look after the little boys?"

"Couldn't I just find another governess for them in Dorchester? Someone a little older perhaps?"

"Ah!" The vicar nodded. "Perchance, are you married?"

"Engaged."

"Tells a lot! The thing is, the boys will need time to adjust to their new life, surely you can understand that. Miss Craig can't just abandon them to you."

"Their new governess and my duchess will learn to take care of them."

"Your grace, please consider. Henry and Stephen have lost the security they knew and they're counting on Miss Craig. It could be terribly damaging for the boys if she was to just suddenly disappear from their lives. If they still lived in their own home, among a familiar environment, it might be easier. However you're not only taking them to a new home, but to a totally new county. It won't hurt you to have a little help from her at the start and after three or so months, you can then release her and bring in someone new."

Errol suddenly brightened up. The vicar was right. The boys would need time to get accustomed to a new governess and their new home, and who better than Miss Lillian Craig to help them do it? "Do you think that will work?"

"Indeed, you have my word on it."

4
NEW HOME, NEW EXPERIENCES

L illian walked around the bedroom that had been allocated to her in the duke's house. It was while they were on their way to Dorchester that she had found out that he was a duke. She'd imagined him to be a baron or marquis, never a duke. Though she was impressed by the title and the man as well, seeing the house in the light of day made her wonder just what had happened to the family money. Perhaps Lord Errol Campbell the Duke of Dorchester was a wastrel who'd squandered the family wealth.

Poor boys, she thought about Stephen and Henry, who were sleeping soundly on the other side of the door. She couldn't believe that she'd been convinced to come to Dorchester, when her intent had been to end up in London and at another job. When she'd mentioned this to Lord Errol, he'd practically begged her to stay with the boys.

She'd only done it because the twins nearly became prostrate with sorrow when she tried to tell them that she would be leaving them. Their uncle had come for them and so they didn't need her anymore. Their wails and screams had ripped through Lilly's heart and they wouldn't be comforted.

"I know that you've probably made other plans for your life, but consider my nephews. They're so attached to you and I believe it would be in their best interests if we slowly weaned them off your affections."

"But I had already promised my new employer that I would join her as soon as I handed the boys over to their guardian, who is you. My work is done."

"I do realize that, Miss Craig," he looked so lost that Lilly's heart was touched. He looked just like her charges when they were begging her not to put them to bed early, or when they wanted some more syrup on their pancakes. Stephen and Henry would be very handsome when they grew up, and for a moment she felt sorrowful that she wouldn't be there to see them grow.

She had come to the Worthingtons through good references from her last employers and she'd hoped that she would be with them for a long while. Being with two very boisterous boys had helped overcome her own pain, caused by the betrayal of one she had loved and trusted. It surprised her that in just three weeks, she'd nearly forgotten about Miles.

His love for a rich older woman had him breaking their engagement off just a few days before their wedding, and getting away from it all had been all she could think of at the time. Now that she'd had a few days to think about it, Miles Brown was a cowardly man who couldn't face her to break off their engagement, instead he'd done it with a hastily written note that had been dropped at her living quarters. As a result she'd been unable to go to work and had begged to be released from her obligations two weeks early. A few weeks earlier she had served her employers with notice of intent to leave them due to her upcoming marriage.

Even now as she closed her eyes and leaned her head against the window, the only face that came up was that of her new employer, the handsome duke. It made her slightly annoyed with herself but she admitted that she'd agreed to the posting only because she didn't immediately want to be parted from the man who made her realize that what she'd felt for Miles was just childish infatuation and not love.

How was it possible that she'd fallen in love with Errol Campbell, a duke, in just three days? Was she mad?

A sound at the doorway made her turn around to find the object of her thoughts observing her with a curious look in his eyes. His cobalt blue intense gaze unnerved her so much that she immediately blushed and turned away. "I'm sorry, your grace. Did you want something?'

"I just wanted to check up on the boys. Have they settled in well?"

"They're fast asleep, your grace."

"That's good, after the excitement of the past few weeks and the long journey from Exeter, the poor fellows must have been exhausted."

"That they were; they barely made it through their dinner and baths before they were out like light."

He stepped further into the room and suddenly Lilly felt as though she couldn't breathe. "And you, Miss Craig? How are you settling in?"

"Alright, your grace. This is a beautiful room and I'm grateful."

"My mother insisted on ensuring that our governesses were well taken care of, just to appease them so they wouldn't leave." Errol picked up a small figurine that was on the mantle. "Alfred and I were very lively children, Stephen and Henry remind me of ourselves when we were their age. I'm amazed at how quickly they have taken to you, given that you only joined their household a few weeks ago."

"They are such delightful boys, very curious and adventurous, but also taking to their lessons with equal passion as they do their play, your grace."

They both turned towards the window when they heard a carriage drawing up to the front of the house. "Well, I will leave you to settle in. Dinner will be brought up to you and the boys, and you'll only join me downstairs when I say so," he saw her pale and felt badly that he had to make such an announcement. But until he was sure about Abby's reception of the twins and their beautiful governess, he wasn't going to risk any shouting matches or tantrums.

He left the room and closed the door gently behind him, pausing for a while to collect himself. Abby was very observant and she would immediately tell something was wrong if he went down without being prepared. From what he'd seen of Miss Lillian Craig, she was a gentle creature and he doubted that she would be any match for his very jealous and over possessive fiancée. There was bound to be trouble the moment Abby set her eyes on Lilly and he wanted to delay their meeting for as long as possible.

But his fiancée had plans of her own! Immediately when she set foot into the house, her demands began. "Where are those children?" tossing her gloves and reticule on the table in the hallway, she walked towards the drawing room. "And don't tell me they're not here, because everyone in the village is talking about them. I want to see them for myself." Which was quite an exaggeration according to Errol, for no one save the servants of his household knew about the children's presence in Dorchester.

"Will you be patient a little while? The poor boys are exhausted after the journey from Exeter, and also given what they've been going through. Their governess will bring them down as soon as they get up, I gave her those instructions."

Errol's words appeased Abby but only for a short time. "I'm going up to see those boys. After all, they've come into our lives and I'll be expected to show some form of interest in them. What better time than now?" And with that, she marched up the stairs and burst into the boy's room where they were just getting up. One look at Lillian, who was helping her charges, and the blood immediately drained from Abbey's face. "Who are you?" She turned to Errol who was behind her. "Who is this woman?"

"This is Miss Lillian Craig, the boys' governess. Miss Lillian, this is Lady Abigail Wentworth, my fiancée." Lillian curtsied.

"Good evening, my lady."

Abby ignored her, glared at the boys who immediately started whimpering and then she flounced out of the room, Errol in hot pursuit. She didn't stop until she had reached the drawing room. "I demand that you send those children and that woman away."

"You know I can't send the boys away, Abby. I discovered that they're my brother's sons."

"You lie," she hissed. "That woman must have cast a spell on you to make you think those boys are related to you."

"Abby," Errol was trying very hard to hold on to his patience. "Stephen and Henry are my nephews and even you can see the likeness. The only reason I brought Miss Lillian was to take care of them is because they got attached to her and it wasn't easy separating them. But rest assured, as soon as I find another governess, she will be leaving."

But Abby was having none of that. She drew her gloves on and gave him a cold look. "You need to make up your mind whether it's me or the boys. I'm not going to take care of someone else's illegitimate brats.

"Don't call them that," Errol frowned. "It's not fair to be angry at little boys who've just lost their mother and the only father they ever knew. Please be patient, my love," he tried to take her hand but she drew away.

"I'm leaving now and won't set foot into this house until you send word that that woman and those boys are no longer living under your roof," she was momentarily overcome by passion and grabbed him. "Send them away, my darling. Can't you see that they're already coming between us, ruining our love?"

"Abby," he patted her arm gently. "Those little boys are innocent of any wrong. I went up to Exeter to find out why Caroline Sanders had named me their guardian and was prepared to place them into a foundling home." He sighed, running a hand through his hair. "The moment I saw them, I knew that they were my brother's sons and there's no way I was going to turn my back on them. Please understand that."

Abby pulled away as if someone had struck her, turning so pale that he feared she might swoon. "Are you alright, why don't you sit down?"

"Don't touch me," she said in a cold voice. "Don't contact me unless you get rid of those people. I'm giving you three days," she said, picking up her reticule.

"My lady," Errol had never addressed Abby in such a manner and she paled once again. "Instead of extending the issue please let me give you my answer here and now." He took a deep breath. "I'll never turn my nephews out of their rightful home, because I know that if it was Alfred in my place right now, he would protect my offspring too. I'm sorry you feel so strongly about them, but they're innocent and harmless children and shouldn't have to lose another home."

"Very well then," she walked stiffly to the door, then turned around. "You'll be hearing from my father," and slammed the door so hard that Errol felt as if his teeth were jarred from the jaw.

5

HERE COMES TROUBLE

Trouble was brewing, and Errol had a feeling that it wasn't going to be something that would quickly pass. Just an hour after Lady Abigail had exited his house in anger, a messenger was sent to deliver a note to him from her father. The footman didn't stay a single minute longer than was necessary and as Errol turned to enter the house, the note in his hand, he saw Lilly standing uncertainly at the top of the stairs. Putting it away, he took long strides towards the staircase.

"Miss Lillian, did you need something from me? Please come down."

Lilly shook her head slightly. "I'd better not leave the boys for too long. It's just that Lady Abigail looked very angry and I was coming down to apologize to her because our presence seems to have unnerved her."

Errol smiled, "Think nothing of it," he joined her and led the way to the nursery. "Let me see how my nephews are doing."

"They were a little shaken at the display of anger," there was a note of recrimination in her voice but when he turned sharply to look at her, all he could see was innocence on her face. "Stephen and Henry haven't been exposed to anger and arguments all their lives, so it's natural for them to react to such."

"Are they alright?"

"I believe so, otherwise I wouldn't have been able to come out to the landing," they'd reached the nursery and Errol paused for a brief moment before opening the door.

"I don't hear any sounds from within."

"That's because they're busy playing with the toys that you so thoughtfully provided for them. They lost all theirs in the fire and it hasn't been easy."

Errol found himself reaching out a hand, touching her soft cheek and in the dim light, thought she blushed. "You've also been through a lot and for that, I'm sorry. Lady Abigail won't be bothering you or the boys again."

"I'm truly sorry to hear that. If you'd like me to speak with her…."

Errol chuckled softly, "Oh, I would love to see that happening, but as I said, it's no bother. What's done is done, and now we have to pay attention to the little ones." He opened the door and the twins immediately looked up and flashed him identical smiles, and it gave him such a warm feeling within that he was glad he'd decided to choose them over Abby.

Ignoring the letter that was burning a hole in his pocket, Errol spent nearly one hour on the floor with the boys and Lilly felt such a deep longing within her. Despite the fact that Lord Campbell had come into fatherhood unexpectedly, he seemed to be taking it all in his stride. He frolicked on the floor with the boys and finally she had to call it a day.

"Time for your snack, story and then bed."

"Miss Lilly can Uncle Errol read us our bedtime story?" Henry was on Errol's back while Stephen was holding the scarf that they'd begged from Lilly, which was what they were using as pretend reins. The duke was supposed to be their pony and they were taking turns riding on his back.

"Please Miss Lilly!" Errol joined in begging the boys and she had to give in to their similar expressions. Errol wasn't good for her health, that much she admitted to herself, but he was a nobleman and she was just the governess. The sooner she got over her silly infatuation of him, the better it would be for everyone. Besides, with the very beautiful and stylish Lady Abigail, she stood no chance at winning the duke's affections. Their quarrel was just temporary and she was sure they would reconcile and probably get married soon. The good thing was that she would be long gone before that happened.

"Alright then, but you have to say your prayers first and then your uncle will read you your bedtime story."

It felt good, that's all Errol thought about as he prepared himself for bed. His personal valet, Robert, was putting his coat away when he exclaimed softly.

"Robert, what's the problem?"

"Your grace, there seems to be some letter or note in your pocket," it was customary for the valet to check all the pockets for any documents or items. He pulled it out and handed it over to Errol.

"Oh dear," Errol sighed. It was the letter from Abby's father that he'd clean forgotten about as he spent at least two hours with the twins. They were delightful children and he found himself silently thanking Carol for giving him this opportunity to be their foster father. Alfred would have loved his sons and for a moment, Errol allowed the grief to wash over him. But not for long for he held a letter that he was almost afraid to open.

Lord Thomas Wentworth was a fine fellow but with only one great weakness. His daughter Abigail. Though only a baron, he'd made his wealth overseas while working for the British Indian Trading Company. He held a lot of clout in society, and crossing him often meant social suicide for the offender. According to Lord Thomas, Abigail was his princess and angel and anyone who wanted to remain in his good graces must literally worship her.

Errol knew that Thomas had accepted his suit because he felt his daughter deserved to be a duchess, even though had he had his way, she would be a member of the royal family. Still, he was generous enough to even give Errol part of the dowry so he could begin renovations on the manor and estate where his princess would be moving to.

"Well, might as well get it over and done with," Errol said as he tore open the expensive envelope and pulled out the bonded and emblazoned writing sheet. One single sheet of paper that he knew was about to change his life forever, and as he perused through it, turned as white as the paper he held and hastily sat down on his bed before he swooned.

"It has come to my attention that the engagement between my daughter Abigail and yourself has been broken due to a misdemeanour. My poor princess is distraught and hasn't eaten since she came home from your house.

In view of this, I will kindly request that you reimburse me the part dowry payment that I have already given to you. This is so I can prepare to find a more suitable husband for my princess. I would appreciate this being done within the next seven days."

The note had no salutation and neither had it been signed, and Errol felt slighted. But what was worse were the implications of the note. Where was he supposed to get nearly ten thousand pounds to give back to the baron? He could perhaps go and plead for more time, but that would be an exercise in futility. The baron wasn't known to be very kind to those who owed him money. If he wanted his money within seven days, then he was going to have his money within seven days. Nothing short of that would appease him. In any case, it would release Errol from the engagement and give him time to concentrate on his nephews and their future. And a certain governess whose face had taken permanent residence in his mind!

6
DESPERATE MEASURES

"Y ou had an affair with Carol, just admit it," Abby screeched, flinging things all around the study. "Why are you denying it and the evidence is clear for everyone to see?

"For the last time, Abby, I didn't have an affair with Carol. I barely knew the woman and at the time she was engaged to my brother, I was only about twenty."

"Men have fathered children even when they're as young as fourteen so that's not an excuse. Just look at how closely those brats resemble you, and now you want to go and lie about it?"

"Clearly, there's no reasoning with you."

"Oh, so now I'm being unreasonable?"

"I didn't mean it that way," Errol was tired of the shouting match, though to his credit, it was Abby doing all the shouting. He was sure the whole of Dorchester could hear her and wondered what they were thinking. Worse, her voice carried and he didn't want to imagine how his nephews were reacting to the disturbance.

Even though returning the dowry had cost him a lot, he was relieved that their engagement was over, now he could go on with his life. The only trouble was that Abigail had insisted on coming back and in her usual selfish way, had overlooked all that her father had put him through.

"You never loved me," she pouted and whereas before he'd thought is somewhat pretty, now all it did was irritate him. "Otherwise you wouldn't have chosen those brats over me."

"Listen, my lady. You chose to end our engagement for a reason I couldn't understand. You were demanding that I choose you over my dead brother's sons and the poor boys have no one else in the world." He shook his head. "You put the advertisement in the newspapers about the end of our engagement, so I don't understand why you came back here again."

Abigail didn't want to imagine that she had actually lost Errol forever. She'd expected him to come crawling back to her when her father sent him the note but none of that happened. Instead, she'd heard from reliable sources that he'd sold some of the family properties to settle the advance dowry her father had demanded back. Still, she'd held on to hope that he would be missing her for she believed that he was quite besotted with her but two weeks down the line, and he'd not as much as sent her a note. It hurt that he would forget all about her but she was sure it all had to do with the new governess.

"It's all about her, isn't it?"

"What's about who?"

"That governess! You're attracted to her and that's why you're passing me over." She stood up. "Well, if you want to embarrass your family name with the servants then go ahead, but I'll not be a part of it."

Errol watched Abby going out and shook his head. The woman was so dramatic and he hoped she would finally leave him alone. He had a lot on his mind, the paramount thing being how he was going to take care of his family. For the short term they would cope, but soon they would be starving if things didn't change.

If Errol thought Abby's screeching was bad, he realized that things were worse when he attended a ball they'd been invited to together and everyone literally turned their noses up at him. He felt uncomfortable when he experienced their whispers and saw their glares.

It became worse when snide remarks passed all over his head and he didn't even last thirty minutes at the ball.

Abigail was the life of the party and he saw her laughing and flirting with a number of young men, some of whom she wouldn't have even greeted before. He knew that it was all a show that had been put on to slight and embarrass him.

Lilly was getting herself some warm milk from the kitchen when she heard a carriage drawing up at the front door. She was aware that the duke was out for one of the many balls that were taking place, and wondered who the visitor could be. Reynolds, the old butler had since retired since his arthritis was acting up and she didn't feel very comfortable opening the door to a stranger at this time of the night.

As she stood in the hallway staring at the massive door, she was surprised when Reynolds dragged himself along the corridor. "It's the master," he said by way of explanation, going on to open the door. Errol strode in, a resigned look on his face.

"I didn't expect anyone to be up at this time," he said after waving at the butler. "Are the boys alright?"

"Yes, your grace." She turned to leave but something held her back. She sighed inwardly and faced him once again. "Is everything alright, your grace?"

"Miss Craig, life is very unfair sometimes, but what to do?"

"Do you want to talk about it?"

He shook his head at first, then nodded. "I'm sorry that my mood is most foul at this hour and please pardon me in advance for any negative reactions. Shall we retire to the drawing room?"

"Yes, my lord."

"Please dispense with all titles from now on, for I don't feel worthy of them."

"It wouldn't be proper, your grace." She followed him to the drawing room and sat down. He took the opposite seat from her and held his head in his hands. From the close distance she could see the tightness around his mouth and knew that he was under much stress.

"It was a most horrible evening," he started. "Never have I been so humiliated and scorned by people who have all along seemed to be friends."

"Was there any reason for that, your grace?"

"Lady Abigail was holding court and from the looks she was throwing me, she must have been spreading rumours. Did you know that she's claiming that I got Lady Carol in the family way and abandoned her?"

"I'm sorry to hear that, your grace."

His lips tightened. "I don't want anyone coming here to make life difficult for my nephews. This is a small village and with all the nasty rumours going around, it's just a matter of time before people start coming here with all manner of reasons. Their main intention will be just to have a look at the boys and see if what Lady Abigail is saying is true."

"You don't have to worry about that, sir. I'll make sure no one has access to the twins, and mercifully we don't have a whole retinue of servants who would make things worse."

"I had to let nearly all of them go because the estate is in a mess and I wasn't able to afford their wages," the sadness in his voice told her that it hadn't been an easy decision for him to make and she found herself respecting him even more. He'd given up his marriage for the two little boys who were now his responsibility and that had greatly moved her. A few days ago when Lady Abigail came to the house, she'd heard the young woman shouting and snuck out of the house with the boys, intending to get them as far away from any disturbances as possible. On their way back, Lady Abby who'd been riding a beautiful mare, had passed them, glared at her with so much dislike that she'd gasped. The woman was trouble for the boys especially, and Lilly wasn't going to give her a chance to harm her charges in any way.

"I'm sorry about that."

He made a sound signifying his impatience. "Would you stop saying that! None of it is your fault," then he waved a hand. "I'm sorry, things have been so difficult these past few days and now with the whole village turning their backs against me, I don't know what to do."

Lilly longed to reach out a hand and wipe his brow but knew that it wasn't proper. She was just a servant and it was even odd for them to be seated together at this late hour, especially since she wasn't appropriately dressed. But she found herself unwilling to leave the poor man alone.

"My lord, what I know about people who like to spread rumours about others is that they're really sad and just lashing out in their pain. Since they're unable to control whatever is happening around them, they usually feel that striking out at others will give them some form of relief."

"And does it?" There was a softness in his eyes that hadn't been there earlier.

"Unfortunately, no. The trouble is that at some point, the truth will come out and then their rumours will be dismissed as falsehoods. What then happens to the person or people is that no one can trust them again, and they end up losing friends."

"Who made you so wise, young lady?"

"I've been governess since I turned eighteen and worked for two families. My first employer was a very wise lady who never let what other people thought about her bother her at all. She lived life on her own terms and people learnt to respect her for it."

"Why didn't you stay with her then?"

Lilly smiled, "I wasn't dismissed with bad behaviour," and his slight flush made her realize that he'd been thinking along those lines. "My employer's family was relocating to Paris, France and I didn't want to go along. So she gave me a good recommendation and that's how I ended up with Lord and Lady Worthington. The Earl worked in the foreign office and got the posting abroad."

"Though Paris might have been a pleasant experience for you, I'm glad you decided not to go." His eyes had an undecipherable message, "My nephews have gained a wonderful governess for I'm sure that not many young ladies would have stayed for three weeks with them under their circumstances."

"That's not true, the boys are so lovely that no one would have just willingly abandoned them."

"You've got a very kind heart that sees the good in people. Sadly though, that's not how life is. What you did for my nephews can only be termed as sacrificial giving. I'm not able to pay you as much as you deserve, but I'm most grateful."

"I better check on the boys now, they have the tendency to call out for me in the night and if I'm not close by, we might be subjected to some yelling."

Errol stood up when Lillian did and stepped closer. He took her hand and she felt her heart beating rapidly. "You're a very precious woman, Miss Craig and I'm happy that you're here."

"Thank you, sir," she said breathlessly. "I have to go now."

"You do that," Errol let her go, for he didn't really trust himself at that moment. The temptation to pull her closer and rest his chin on the top of her head was great, but he didn't want to frighten her away. The boys and by extension Lilly Craig were the only ones who made his life worthwhile. He watched as she hurried out of the room, then sat down once again and held his head in his hands. What was he going to do about his complex situation?

7
SEEKING REFUGE

"Miss Craig, I've summoned you here at this late hour because I'd like to tell you that things are really getting out of hand here in Dorchester," Errol paced the length of his study. "It's getting so bad that even some of my tenants are joining in, which means I'm losing the respect I had with my people. That's the worst thing anyone should ever have to endure, loss of respect from one's own subjects."

"I'm very sorry that things are so bad, my lord." He'd woken her up in the wee hours of the morning.

"The best solution is for us to leave for London immediately. Our family house isn't the best because it's in an old part of the city, at least we shall have some respite there."

"What will happen to the estate?"

"One or two loyal servants will take care of things until we're able to return, which I hope will be someday soon." He paused and put his hands in his pockets. "My brother Alfred and I always said that we would never bring our children up in London, and that's what I really want for these boys. They have to know that they're responsible for the tenants on the estate and they can only learn that by living among their people. London has its attractions but any good landlord knows that for his estate to flourish, he has to be present most of the time."

"Lady Carol loved the countryside," Lilly said. "When I joined her household, she told me that she loved Sleepers' Haven because it was so far removed from the loud towns and that was where she wanted her sons to be brought up. She also talked of taking them to Eton when they were older," her tone fell. "It's so sad that she won't be here to see what fine boys her sons will grow up to be."

"I'll honour her memory and also my brother's by being a good guardian to the boys. They love you so much and my prayer is that you'll be with us for a long time."

"I'll have to leave some day, when you get a duchess. Her ladyship may have her own ideas of a governess for the boys. In the meantime, I'll do my best for them, sir."

"That's all I ask."

If Errol thought that by fleeing Dorchester the rumours would stop, he was grossly mistaken. As soon as he arrived in London, he was summoned to the Regent's court and that's when he knew that he was in trouble.

The Regent wouldn't even see him, but asked Lord Phillip Cobble, the Chancellor of the Duchy of Lancaster to conduct the interview or more like an interrogation. He was considered the Regent's right hand man and being in his good graces would be advantageous for Errol and his estate.

"Errol," the middle aged man stretched his hand out when Errol was announced into his office. "It's good to see you boy, and I was very sorry to learn of your father's untimely death. Lord George was a good man."

"Thank you, sir, you're very kind." Though Lord Phillip was his peer, Errol respected him first because of his age and also because of his position. The chancellor was being very generous with his words because everyone knew that Errol's father, the late duke had been a gambler and an alcoholic who squandered his estate. Errol always excused his behaviour because his father had gone to pieces when his mother died. He'd never recovered nor stopped grieving for her.

"Please sit, would you like anything to drink?" He rang the small bell and a servant came in.

Errol was thirsty but he didn't want to choke on anything. He was so nervous that he wasn't sure his hands could hold anything steadily. But it would be considered rude for him to decline, so he nodded. "A cup of tea, thank you."

Lord Phillip watched the young man and sympathized with him. He really was a good sort of fellow, quiet and hardworking if what he'd heard was true, but the rumours had to be looked into. The Prince Regent was seeking men of good repute to add to his panel of advisors and they'd been considering the Duke of Dorchester when someone mentioned that things weren't going so well with him.

Once the tea was served and the servants had left, Lord Phillip cleared his throat. He was known to be a very straightforward man who never beat around the bush. "Some nasty rumours have reached the Regent's ears and I wanted to find out what is really happening. What's going on, Errol?"

"My lord, if it has to do with the children in my care, I'd like to say that it's an unfortunate incident, sir."

"What do you mean?"

"Six years ago, my brother Alfred was engaged to Lady Caroline Sanders and just a few days before their wedding, she called it off and soon married Lord Brian Worthington. They moved to Sleepers' Haven where they lived relatively quiet lives and soon after, my brother died under tragic circumstances. When Lady Caroline broke off their engagement, he was so distraught that he took to the bottle. Just a few weeks ago, I received a letter from the Vicar of Sleepers' Haven, informing me that Lady Carol had appointed me as her sons' guardian in the event of her death. I traveled to Exeter and was shocked to find that the twins resembled my late brother. That's when the vicar told me that her ladyship had confessed to him that the boys were my brother's offspring. Apparently, when she discovered that she was with child and informed him, he wasn't immediately receptive and she didn't want to bring shame to her family name, so she accepted Lord Brian's suit."

"So the rumours that you had an adulterous affair with a married woman and sired her children isn't true?"

"It isn't true, my lord."

Lord Phillip grunted softly. "I'll have to look into all this and inform the Regent accordingly. Meanwhile, keep a low profile and this will soon blow over. The truth has a way of coming out in the end, so have no fear. You'll be vindicated one day soon. And in any case, what does it matter? You're now the father of those two boys, even though in your case you were shoved into unexpected fatherhood." He rubbed his chin thoughtfully. "Am I to deduce then that your engagement to Lady Abigail Wentworth is now over?"

"Yes, sir. It's unfortunate that my lady and I won't be getting married after all."

"You're both still young and I'm sure you'll make good matches in the end."

"That's very kind of you to say, sir."

Even though he'd found a gentle ear with the chancellor, Errol was still upset about the rumours and especially because they'd followed them to London. He couldn't go anywhere without someone raising the issue. But when Lilly returned from an outing to the park with the boys one morning, looking clearly upset, he knew it was time to put a stop to everything.

"What happened?"

Lilly shook her head and pointed at the boys with her chin. Errol nodded; she didn't want the children upset and he respected that. But he wasn't about to let it go so he waited until he was sure that she had put the boys down for the night and sent his valet to fetch her from her room.

"My lord, you sent for me?"

"Indeed I did," he sat down in the shabby chair in his small study. He missed Dorchester because he didn't much like the small town house. It was supposed to be just a temporary dwelling place when he was in London on business, not a long term abode. "Now please tell me why you were so upset this morning."

"It's really nothing."

"You can't say that and yet someone clearly offended you. Don't worry, I won't go to their doorstep and challenge them to a duel, if that's what you fear." Lilly smiled and he nodded. "That's more like it. Now tell me."

"The boys and I were in the park when three or four women came up to us and started asking me very disturbing questions. They made a lot of insinuations and I'm afraid I may have been rather rude to them, before bringing the boys home."

"I just wish I knew who they were, but have no fear, they will soon send their notes of complaints to the house." He rested his elbows on the desk and held his head. "Will this nightmare never end?"

"I should have been more careful and polite, sir. I'm sorry."

"Don't ever apologize for defending your charges, Miss Craig. In any case, they attacked you first. Just try to keep your head down."

"We'll only play in the backyard from now on, so that we don't have to meet with nasty people like those again."

"Good girl." He leaned back and a faraway look came into his eyes. "I wish I could take you and the boys and flee into exile, and return many years from now when all these nasty rumours have ended."

Lilly shook her head. "That would be a very unwise thing to do, my lord."

"You think so?"

"I know so. Rumours are like a blazing fire when they happen, but at some point even the fiercest of fire dies down. Something else will come up and people will forget all about this family. You just need to bear it for a few more days and then all will be well."

"You're sure?"

"I've lived in London most of my life and I know it for a fact. Many people are idle and need something to do, so they find joy in spreading nasty rumours. But soon, some other scandal comes up and they move on. My lady used to refer to rumour mongers as locusts that invade a place, sweep it clean and move on. She would say that even though locusts devastated the land, there was always the hope for a new beginning. So, even though this family will be hurt by the rumours, there's hope for newness again. You'll be vindicated, my lord."

8
NEWNESS OF LIFE

He was in love and though it frightened him a little, it also made him smile. For the first time in his life, Errol Campbell was really in love. And with his nephews' governess of all people! He could just imagine what London would have to say to that.

A few months ago, he may have scoffed at the idea of a nobleman like him falling in love with a commoner but now that it had happened to him, he understood. Love had no bounds and could strike anyone. In his case, it had happened subtly without his being aware of it. Spending time with Lilly and the boys because they were practically under house arrest for a few weeks made him finally admit that she was the woman he wanted by his side forever. She never complained even when their fare wasn't all that pleasant. She taught the boys how to sing and laugh and he began doing the same too.

Just like she'd predicted, a new scandal soon had the attention diverted to the new unfortunate subjects. A marquis, married and the father of four sons had put his wife's sister in the family way and the two ladies were tearing each other to shreds in public.

When he told Lilly of the incident, she shook her head sadly, "It's terrible for sisters to do that to each other. Their fight is being fuelled by opportunists but they're too blinded by anger to see that. I just pray that they will soon come to their senses and mend their torn relationship before it's too late."

Lilly was really an angel, his angel. The past few weeks would have been unbearable without her but she found a way of making him smile. He needed to tell her that he loved her, praying that she wouldn't bolt. He was sure that she loved him though she was probably intimidated by his title and position. Reaching for the small bell on the table at his side, he rang it and she soon appeared. Since the only other servants present in the house were elderly, Lilly had taken over some of the work too.

"My lord?"

"Please come in and sit down."

Lilly's heart was pounding. Had she done something wrong? Lord Errol rarely summoned her unless there was a matter to be discussed. But he looked almost happy and her heartbeat slowed down somewhat. "Yes, your grace?"

Errol stood up and came around his desk, sitting on the chair opposite hers. He reached out for her hands. "I'm sure you know what I want to tell you."

She shook her head. "No," but it came out all hoarse, causing him to chuckle softly.

"My dear girl, you're blushing so delightfully," he rubbed the backs of her hands with his thumbs. "I don't like to prolong matters so I'll just say it. I love you, Lillian Craig. I've fallen in love with you."

'Oh!"

"Is that all you can say?" He smiled gently at her.

"My lord…."

"Errol."

"Errol."

"I like how you say my name." He raised her hands and kissed them both. "You were saying something?"

"Errol, your station and mine are so different. What will people say?"

"Haven't you been the one who keeps telling me that I shouldn't worry what people will say? Dear heart, you've made me see that it's not about titles and society, but about you and me. I know that I don't want to spend another day without you in my life."

"We barely know each other."

"Excuses my love?" He leaned forward and brushed his lips gently against hers. "I know that I'm in love with you and people have already said the worst they can about me, about us. What matters is how we feel about each other." He raised her chin. "Do you have feelings for me little one?"

Tears welled up in her eyes and he pulled her into his arms and Lilly soon found herself seated on his lap. "Don't cry."

"I don't know what to say."

"That you love me and once you say it, you'll feel better."

Lilly was deeply in love with the duke and she'd wept into her pillow many nights at the hopelessness of it all. Now to find that he loved her was too much and she didn't know how to react to it all. It made her so happy but also humbled her that such a man as the duke would be willing to come down to her level.

"What are you thinking?"

"It's humbling that you would come down to your handmaid's level, my lord."

"Lilly, man is created equal but situations cause us to be born in different stations. The wonder of life is that the base born and the nobles are conceived in the same way, born in the same way and though they live differently, will all die and descend into the earth. We come with nothing in this world and though we eventually possess much, when we leave, we leave naked as we came. It's a humbling thought. Love happens to kings and paupers, princes and vagabonds, and everyone else in between; not that I'm referring to you in a derogatory manner."

"I understand what you're saying."

"Please put me out of my misery dear girl. Tell me that you love me and my heart will settle down."

She smiled so sweetly at him that it caught his breath. This woman was so lovely and innocent, yet there was an underlying strength within her that made him know he'd received a great blessing. By falling in love with her, he knew that he'd made the right choice. "Yes, Errol, I do love you so very much."

9

IT ALL ENDS WELL

"Will you stand still, Stephen," Errol's voice was full of exasperation and the little boy giggled. His brother was seated quietly on the bed watching them. "If the two of you want to see me married to my beloved Lillian today, then you have to stand still as I tie this cravat around your little neck."

"Cravat, cravat," Henry chanted out the new word.

"Yes, and in a few years time you'll be tying your own and going out to dazzle the poor ladies."

"Uncle Errol?"

"Yes Stephen?"

"If you marry Miss Lillian, will she become our mother?"

"Yes, dear boy."

"And you will be our father?"

Errol nearly choked on the lump that welled up in his throat. He'd longed for the day when the boys would see him as their father and not merely their uncle. "Yes," he said in a hoarse voice. The wisdom of five years olds!

"Uncle Errol," Henry piped up. "Can we start calling you papa today?"

"Come here," he held out his hands and hugged the two boys tightly, blinking rapidly so the tears wouldn't fall. "I love you both so much and it will be an honour if you called me Papa or Father."

Lilly was a radiant bride and once again, Errol found himself fighting back his tears. Love had a way of turning a man's insides all mushy and he knew that for as long as he lived, he would love this woman and these two boys who'd brought so much joy into his life. He'd told her that he had nothing to offer her except his heart and love, and she'd responded by telling him that it was all that she wanted and had prayed for. He was indeed a very blessed man.

Theirs was a simple wedding for they didn't have much, but the love they shared was so great that it superseded anything else. They returned to a simple meal prepared by the cook and as they were about to sit down and partake of it, the door bell rang.

"I'll get it," Errol stood up for he'd given his valet and butler the day off so he could be alone with his bride. He returned a few minutes later holding a thick envelope in his hand. "Someone just delivered this, and it's from Littleton and Applegate Solicitors. Never heard of them."

"There's only one way to find out, open it."

Errol opened the envelope with trembling hands, expecting to find a summons to appear or show cause why legal action shouldn't be taken against him. He read the first few sentences and sat down heavily, a stunned look on his face.

"What is it, my love?" Lilly was immediately at his side. "What do they want?"

"These solicitors represent the late Lord Brian Worthington. Apparently, they've been looking for me because of his estate."

"Lord Worthington's estate was all destroyed in the fire."

"No, that was just one of his properties. The man was very wealthy and yet lived very simply. According to this letter, he had vast business interests in India and had been in the process of winding up his affairs when the tragedy befell him and his wife. Carol and these boys were named as his sole heirs and in the event of their deaths, the person named as the boys' guardian would be their trustee."

"Oh!"

"Lord Worthington was a very wealthy man and the solicitors have asked me to present myself at their offices with the boys, so they can hand everything necessary over to me. There's a town house mentioned in Regent Square too."

"Oh my!" Lilly had passed by the square on one of her hurried trips to church but without the boys of course, and had admired the beautiful houses which belonged to the wealthy families of London.

Errol looked at his nephews who were unaware of what was going on, happily eating their simple meal. They were his family now and he'd been vindicated.

"You and these little ones have brought me so much grace and blessings, Lilly." He stood up and pulled her close. "You're my angels. Now we've been vindicated for the letter states that as guardian and trustee, there's a large sum I'm to receive to see to my own affairs so that I'll be able to concentrate on the boys."

"Lord Brian was a worthy man though I didn't know him for long."

"He must have loved Carol to do this for her and her sons."

"Love has a way of wanting to do the best for others."

And Errol silently agreed for he'd prayed to find a way to show Lilly how much he loved her by providing well for her and his nephews. Now he could do it without any strain and finally he was free.

"Right at this moment I wish you could tear my heart open and see the love that is in there for you."

"You're making me feel very self conscious, my lord."

"I'm your husband and you still call me by title."

"Errol," Lilly smiled. She was loved and she loved back. This thing called love was wonderful and she prayed that she would make her lord and husband happy for the rest of her life. Errol was thinking the very same thing and in years to come, that's exactly what they did.

TAMING THE LADY

CLEAN REGENCY ROMANCE

1
FROM GRACE TO GRASS

"**I** could just scream," Lady Abigail Wentworth clenched her teeth in frustration. She hurled her hair brush across the room, hitting and cracking the mirror on the opposite wall. That only made her angrier and soon her bedroom resembled a battle field.

"How could he do this to me," she screamed at no one in particular because the servants in her father's house knew to keep their distance when she was in one of her rages. "Who does that man think he is, duke or not. He will pay for this slight against my family name," she finished by throwing herself across her bed. She sobbed for a moment, wondering what had gone wrong with her life.

One moment, she was telling everyone about her upcoming wedding, and the next moment she was cancelling the engagement. She was now the laughing stock of Dorchester County for everyone said she couldn't hold on to a fiancé, let alone a husband.

Lord Errol Campbell had chosen his brother's illegitimate sons over her and it hurt deeply. She'd thought that the man was ensnared and enraptured with her, but she'd been wrong. All was going well until those blasted children came into Errol's life.

"Aargh!" Her fists pummelled the pillow. "Why did those boys have to come into our lives?" By now she would have been married to the most handsome man in Dorchester, if not the whole of England but here she was, unmarried and all alone. She couldn't imagine that her beloved Errol would eventually belong to another woman, that governess no doubt. It infuriated her that a little miss nobody was going to take her place and become a duchess.

There was a knock at her door and she ignored it at first, but the person persisted. "Come in," she screamed and the door opened to reveal a middle aged man with a shock of white hair on his head. "Oh Papa," she scrambled off the bed and into his arms. "I'm so sad."

"My princess," he held her close. "Do you need some more money for shopping, or shall I take you to Paris?" Lord Thomas Wentworth loved his daughter, perhaps too much as his wife had complained years ago. But his little girl was motherless now and he did all he could to make sure she was happy. She was his only child and his world.

"Papa," she pulled back. "It's not always about money, shopping and trips," she said.

"What does my little princess want? Mention anything and I'll get it for you."

"Oh Papa," she sank down on her bed. "I want Errol."

"My love, he doesn't deserve you for the way he treated you. You'll find a good man who will treat you right and will be worthy of you. Now, cheer up and come with me to the theatre. There's a good girl and your papa won't take no for an answer. Shall I send for a new gown for you, my dear?"

"Oh Papa, it's too late for a new gown now."

Lieutenant David Birch's right leg hurt so badly that he nearly passed out from the pain, but he grit his teeth and lowered himself to the ground, leaning against a fencing post. He was here but the effort of rising up and getting to the gate and beyond was more than he could manage so he just sat and rubbed his leg, moaning softly.

Desperation had made him take this journey back home, even though he'd vowed never to return to the one place that gave him a lot of pain especially these past few years. Losing his mother three years ago was the worst thing he'd ever gone through and he didn't think he would get over it. When he lost his father just two months later, life had changed drastically for the young man. That meant his brother Edward had taken over as the Duke of Somerset. Being the second son, he was glad his father had bought him a commission in the army as he didn't stand to inherit anything and had to make his own way in life.

He closed his eyes tiredly, willing the pain to subside so he could make his way to the house where he doubted that he would be welcome. Since he had nowhere to go, he would bear with his sister-in-law's snide remarks about him; just as long as they gave him a roof and something to eat once in a while. He needed a little time to recuperate and rest his injured leg. Once he was up and around again, he would be gone from their lives for good.

Lately, he'd been toying with the idea of asking for a posting to the colonies abroad so that he didn't have to put up with his relatives. It was sad that Edward was his only sibling and yet they'd never got along from when they were young. Sometimes, David was tempted to blame his parents for his brother's haughtiness. From when Edward could walk, their parents had made him aware that he was to be the next duke and treated him as such, expecting everyone else to do the same. Even David was forced to follow suit such that by the time they were teenagers, Edward treated him worse than even the servants.

David had begun rebelling silently but since he didn't want to hurt his mother's feelings, had borne the treatment in silence. But when his mother died and Edward didn't even come for the funeral, citing other personal interests, his father finally admitted that perhaps they'd done a poor job of raising the next Duke of Somerset. He was selfish and cared nothing for anyone else save his beautiful new bride. David tried to get his brother to pay attention to whatever was going on at the estate but by then it was too late. Edward instead started making unreasonable demands on his father, who was grieving for his beloved wife. The young man didn't seem to notice their father's failing health and it was left to David to do all he could to smooth things over.

Mercifully, just two weeks before his death, the duke had bought David an army commission and the latter was glad to leave home, only returning to bury his father a few days later. For two years, David hadn't been home and he wondered how his brother was faring with his new bride, Lady Camille.

From the moment David had met Camille, just a short time before their mother passed away, he felt that she was more of a social climber than anything else. She was the daughter of a baron but her father didn't have money or influence. Camille had wheedled her way into Edward's life and because she was beautiful, he had succumbed to her charms. Edward loved showing off and having one of the most beautiful women in England as his wife, thinking it made him welcome in many households.

David sighed and struggled to his feet, favouring his injured leg. The doctor who had removed the shrapnel from his leg had advised him to use a walking stick but he didn't want anyone considering him an invalid. He would walk again, even if it was the last thing he ever did.

One of the servants spotted him as he walked up the driveway and came running to help him with his small valise. "Master David, welcome home."

"Thank you, Lionel," he was trying hard not to show that he was in pain, even though his face was pale from the effort of walking. "How is everybody at home?"

"My lord and lady are out for the weekend," the servant said. "They went to the coast for some sunshine because his grace has been feeling poorly lately."

It was the best news David could have received. "When will my brother be back?"

"The duchess said they would return on Tuesday in the afternoon."

"Very well then," David was so happy. He would have at least three days of uninterrupted bliss on the estate before his sister-in-law came and would probably drive him out. She had once told him that he was a burden to the estate and should find somewhere to go. Well, he would rest as much as possible for three days and by the time they returned, would have decided what to do with his life.

2
THE SHOCKING TRUTH

"**D**on't you think you've taken things too far, Abby?" Lady Lucy Biddlecombe asked her friend. They were age mates but the former was married to a marquis. She was a pretty looking lady who seemed to be settling down well in her new role as a wife.

"I haven't done enough, Lucy," Abby hissed. "Errol made me the laughing stock of Dorchester and he thinks he can just get away with it? I'll show him that he made a big mistake when he took in his brother's brats."

Lucy shook her head slowly. "Let it go, will you? There are many other young men who are quite interested in you and they're all unencumbered by family ties. Leave Errol alone, for if you're not aware, he got married about three weeks ago."

"What?" That was news to Abby. "Who did he marry? I didn't read about it in the papers." Abby was so shocked and dismayed but didn't want Lucy to know how deeply her words had affected her. She couldn't believe that Errol was gone from her life for good. It couldn't be true, there must be some mistake. "Are you sure of what you're saying, Lucy?"

Lucy nodded. "They had a private wedding and I understand he married the young lady who was taking care of his nephews."

"That common nobody?"

Lucy observed her friend for a while, feeling sorry for her. The so called 'nobody' had married one of the most handsome and distinguished men in England, but she was wise enough not to make that comment out loud. "In any case, they're married."

"Society will reject him," it stung that Errol could have cast her aside for a mere governess. "What kind of marriage will they have anyway? She's so poor and has nothing, and Errol also has nothing. His estate is dilapidated and he needs to marry someone with money."

"Well, let's stop talking about those two," Lucy changed the subject because she didn't want to tell her friend that the people she despised were now doing very well. Because of the twins, Errol was now able to restore his estate. He had moved his family into the town house left by Lord and Lady Worthington since he was their legal guardian. It was one of those houses that everyone admired and wanted to receive an invitation to, but so far the Duke and Duchess of Dorchester weren't entertaining. They preferred to lead a quiet life away from the limelight. Lucy didn't blame them for one moment, for they had suffered when terrible rumours were going around London about them.

Now, they kept mostly to themselves and even though a few patrons had started inviting them to functions, they were very selective. That made people all the more curious about the couple. Errol defended and protected his wife from society and getting them to open up was going to take a while. Lucy wouldn't have minded being counted among their acquaintances for it was rumoured that the Worthingtons had been very wealthy. Now that Errol was the boys' guardian and trustee of their parents' estate, he was no doubt handling big business. More than that, Daniel her own husband had informed her that the Prince Regent was considering adding Errol Campbell to his list of personal advisors which meant great favour indeed.

Abbey would have been one of those duchesses that society admired and invitations to her balls and parties would have been much sought after. That usurper had taken her place and she wasn't going to let things go as Lucy expected her to. Errol belonged to her and she would do all she could to get him back.

75

"If I want to, I can snatch Errol back from that commoner," Abby said haughtily. "After all, he was deeply in love with me," she raised her nose up and Lucy sighed inwardly. She'd met Errol and his new wife, Lillian at the Regent's court and had been struck at how much in love they were. Though Lady Lillian was simple, she was elegant and what really made Lucy pay attention to the couple was that Errol was genuinely happy. No pretentiousness and false airs, he looked really contented. Errol could barely let his wife out of his sight and when they looked at each other, their love was palpable.

"Do you really want to do that?" She didn't want her friend humiliated for that was bound to happen if she pursued her current course of action.

"Why not? Errol was mine and I want him back."

"Weren't you the one who broke off the engagement because of his nephews? In any case, Errol is now well placed because of those two boys. Perhaps you're now regretting why you acted hastily."

"Don't say that, Lucy," Abby knew her friend was right but she didn't want to hear the words said out loud. "If Daniel had brought in some children from nowhere, would you have agreed to marry him?"

"I would have found out more first, before rejecting the children and subsequently him," Lucy retorted.

"You're a better person than me, Lucy," Abby saw that her friend wasn't too pleased at her comment and wanted to calm her down. Truthfully, Lucy was the only close friend she had as she felt everyone else was judging her for not being married. "Will you help me get Errol back?"

"No, my dear. Daniel would be most annoyed if I tried to run interference in other people's lives. You know how strict my husband is."

"You don't have to tell him anything."

Lucy shook her head. "You know that I could never hide anything from my husband." Lord Daniel Biddlecombe, was one of the Prince Regent's close aides and a very serious individual, but loving towards his wife. Lucy was in love with her husband and never wanted to anger or disappoint him in any way. "Please, for your own sake just let Errol be. Daniel said he's able to introduce you to some fine young men. We're having Percy and his sisters over for lunch this coming Sunday, why don't you come and meet him?"

"Are you by any chance referring to Percival Eldridge the son of a merchant?"

"You say it like it's a bad thing. He comes from the gentry class and their family is very wealthy, Abby. Percy and Daniel were at Eton together and my husband says he's a wonderful man and has asked about you once or twice."

"Why would I want to marry someone who has no title?" Abby scoffed and Lucy felt pity for her delusional friend. When would Abby grow up?

It took him only twenty four hours to decide what he was going to do, but David stayed in the family manor until Tuesday when his brother and sister-in-law returned. Though Edward pretended to be glad to see him, Camille didn't waste any emotions on him.

"So you decided that this is where you want to come and recuperate?" She asked unkindly. "Well, we're expecting guests and have no room."

David nearly laughed out loud but kept a straight face. "I'm sorry, is this any way to welcome your long lost brother-in-law back, dear sister?"

Camille curled her upper lip in disdain. "How much money do you want this time?"

"Just a little to help me find some rooms and be out of your hair," he didn't want to reveal his plans to his family because he felt that they didn't deserve any explanation from him.

"I'll see to it," she said. "Just don't become a bother to your brother. He hasn't been well lately and I don't want him stressed at all."

David nodded, watching as his sister-in-law left the drawing room. He turned to look at his brother who had been quiet during their exchange. Edward looked a little pale and there was something like regret in his eyes.

"You look poorly; didn't spending a few days at the coast do you any good?"

"I'll be alright," Edward said breathlessly, his voice raspy. David frowned. His brother didn't look well at all. He seemed to be under some stress but experience had taught David not to bother asking for he wouldn't receive a satisfactory answer.

"Has the doctor seen you?"

"Camille thinks it's just something that will soon clear up. Frankly, I don't see the need of troubling myself to bring in the doctor when it will pass. Must be the chills or something minor like that."

David wanted to argue but thought better. After all, his brother was an adult and if he chose not to see a doctor for his ailment, who was he to try and insist?

Edward cleared his throat. "I'm sorry about Camille, but she's invited her friends and family for two weeks and we don't have much room."

"Don't worry yourself, brother. I've always taken care of myself and will be alright. All I need is some money to tide me over for the next few weeks as I recuperate. The doctor in Paris told me to rest this leg as much as possible and I can't go out in search of work, much as I'd like to. So, if it's possible for you to give me something little to add to the pension that I receive, I'll be very grateful."

"I'll ask Camille to give you some money."

"Thank you," David turned to leave the room.

"Wait," Edward called out and he turned. "When do you think you'll be gone?" He laughed embarrassedly. "I don't want to hurry you, but everything has to be perfect for this visit."

"Very well, I'll be gone first thing tomorrow morning."

"That's good. I'll make sure Camille settles you with something before you leave."

David just nodded and turned away, and missed seeing the sadness in his brother's eyes.

3

PRIDE COMES BEFORE A DOWNFALL

"I don't believe it," Lucy said breathlessly, staring at the large diamond ring on Abby's finger. "Count Emile Martineau, London's most sought after bachelor."

Abby was glowing; she couldn't believe that she had managed to get the handsome and dandy French nobleman to propose to her. They'd met at Almack's courtesy of one of the patronesses. Abby held an annual voucher which her father had purchased for her and she felt that she had met the right man for her. Errol paled in comparison to the fiery French man who made her feel breathless all the time. It didn't matter that he was much older than she was, actually it added to the allure of their relationship.

Women envied her and men strove to emulate the Frenchman who was one of the best dressed men of the season. He was flamboyant and when he had singled her out, Abby had been thrilled but remembered what Lucy had told her some time ago. *"When you meet a man who catches your eye, don't act silly and childish like the other young women. Be aloof and let him pursue you. It will make him the more determined to win your hand. That's what I did and see how I married one of the best men in England."*

So, Abby had acted aloof and when Emile wouldn't stop pursuing her, she'd known Lucy was right. Within days, he announced that he was completely besotted and love sick and his flowery poems convinced her that she had indeed found herself a worthy partner.

"When is the wedding?"

"Emile doesn't want to wait for long," Abby had stars in her eyes and Lucy was slightly concerned. Like any other female, she appreciated Emile's looks and manner of dressing but he seemed to be too good to be true. "Emile says he'll die of love if I keep him waiting any longer."

"Have you met any of his family yet?"

"When we're married, we will make the trip to Normandy where his family is waiting for us." She grabbed Lucy's hands. "Oh Lucy, I'm so happy," she was smiling broadly. "Emile is such a handsome man, he's rich and just makes my heart melt within me."

"Be careful and guard your virtue," Lucy warned. "Don't get so carried away that you give in to his seduction."

"I would never do that," Abby said indignantly and for that, Lucy was glad. She'd seen many young girls and some of her friends included, succumbing to a man's wiles and things didn't end very well for them. A few had to elope to Gretna Green before evidence of their indiscretions came to light and their marriages weren't happy ones.

"Be very careful not to allow the gentleman to seduce you. You're young and he's mature and very experienced in these matters. Don't let your guard down even for a moment."

"I promise you that I won't."

Abby was to remember her friend's words later and was most grateful that with all her foolishness, her virtue had remained intact. Emile had tried to make her give in to his charm but on that she'd held firm. Believing herself to be so much in love, she hadn't questioned when he insisted on meeting her father and charming his way into the baron's good graces.

Because Abby didn't like bothering herself with serious matters, saying it was men's domain, she was happy to let Emile spend a lot of time with her father while she shopped for her trousseau. Everything had to be perfect for her wedding day and she'd thought she was the luckiest girl alive when Emile threw a very lavish engagement party for her. To be honest, her father had met the expenses of the engagement because Emile said his money was tied up in his bank in Paris. He had promised to reimburse all expenses as soon as the bank cleared his funds. That alone should have alerted Abby to the fact that all was not well but she was too caught up in the euphoria of her upcoming society wedding to pay attention to her intuition.

Everyone who was somebody was invited to the engagement party and her father was so happy. To slight Errol and his ordinary wife, Abby had announced to all and sundry that they'd practically begged her for an invitation. And then her world came crashing down just days later.

Now as she sat beside her father's casket, tears pouring down her eyes, Abby couldn't believe just how terribly things had gone. It had taken Emile Martineau three days to destroy their lives and she didn't know how she was going to ever face anyone in society again.

Two days before her much publicized wedding, Abby had gone to seek out her beloved at his rooms at the Grand Royal Hotel on Regency Street and received the shock of her life. He had fled sometime in the night, taking all her jewels with him. The previous day, he'd asked to see them and claimed that they were dull and needed polishing. In love and fully trusting him, Abby had handed over all her precious jewels as well as those inherited from her mother and grandmother. Now Emile was nowhere to be found and she realized that she'd been the victim of a master conman. How hadn't she seen through his mask?

What made her breakdown further, was coming home that same day to find her father looking as white as a sheet. He was holding some documents in his hands and his solicitor was present.

"Abby, you've killed me," he'd said hoarsely before crumbling to the ground in a dead faint. He never recovered and six hours later, the doctor pronounced him dead.

In the time that her father was unconscious and being attended to by his personal physician, Abby had found out from Mr. Pearson the solicitor that Emile had convinced her father to invest heavily in his ventures. He'd even taken out a huge overdraft from the bank to finance some of those ventures.

"That man promised your father wealth beyond anything he'd ever seen, and I'm afraid, Lord Wentworth put everything he owned into those shady ventures."

It was like being caught up in a horrible dream and overnight, Abby's safe and secure world was no more. Creditors had swarmed the house and she watched in disbelief as everything of value, including her family home was taken over in order to settle her father's debts.

"You have less than a week to find somewhere to live," the solicitor had told her just that morning as she prepared her father's body for burial. "This house now belongs to someone else."

It was a cold and rainy afternoon when Lord Thomas Wentworth was laid to rest beside his wife in the family tomb and Abby felt that her own life was also over. The people who attended her father's burial seemed to be mocking her and she couldn't trust anyone ever again. They were laughing at her and others blamed her for her father's death. Even Lucy who'd hitherto been close to her, hurried away after the burial, clearly not wanting to spend a single moment longer with her.

It hurt and Abby just wanted to die. How could she face society again, knowing that her own foolishness had brought about this catastrophe? Her beloved father had died, when it had emerged that the investments he'd made weren't even worth the paper they were written on. Emile had wiped them clean and left them holding ashes in their hands.

What was she going to do now?

4

SURPRISING EVENTS

D avid sat in the small inn reading news of the latest scandal that had rocked London. The effects were reverberating all around the country and people were stunned at how a noble woman had been deceived by a conman and lost all her inheritance.

"Lady Abigail Wentworth," David twisted his lips. Fate had played a cruel trick on the woman but she deserved what had come to her, he thought. Just a few weeks before, he'd read about his good friend and school mate and the shame that had come to his family after Lady Abigail broke off their engagement.

Lord Errol Campbell had been scorned by society and David had hurt for his friend. When he sent him a note to console him, Errol had written and told him that out of the shame and pain, he'd found true love and he was married to one of the most beautiful and kind women in the whole world. Her name was Lillian and when he came to London, would he look in on them?

David didn't want to face his friends while his own life was lying in tatters. He didn't want to see their pitying looks or the long awkward silences as people desperately thought about what to say. No, he wasn't going to let anyone pity him because he was determined to make it in life. He had his army pension and though little, it would tide him for a long time.

Leaving the family estate a few weeks ago because of his sister-in-law, he'd rented two rooms at a small but comfortable inn and his leg was healing nicely. Camille had given him a few pounds and he'd accepted the offering with gratitude and left home, promising that the next time he returned, he would be a successful man. He would go to the colonies and make his fortune, then return and buy an estate and settle down. That was his dream.

He read the article once again and felt something like pity for Lady Abigail. The tabloids called her proud and arrogant, putting her in a terrible light. He wondered where she was and what she was doing because her family home and other properties had been repossessed to settled the huge debt that her father owed the bank. Apparently, Lord Wentworth had borrowed heavily from the bank to invest *'in mere air'* as one tabloid put it.

A French man had conned the Wentworths and they'd lost all their wealth, and the poor baron had also lost his life as a result of the shock he suffered. It was a terrible situation to be in and for a moment, David actually felt sorry for Lady Abigail. What was she going to do now? Then he shrugged, it was none of his business as he had his own issues to think about.

Living in the inn and getting additional treatment for his leg had eaten into whatever little money he had and he knew that he had to find a way out of London before he became the next scandal for inability to pay for his bed and board.

He sat lost in his thought, his memories taking him to happier times when he was younger and without a care in the world. Errol had made life so interesting for him, for he would insist on David accompanying him to their estate in Dorchester, where they would run wild and free, ride as much as they wanted and just enjoy life. They'd had good times and the last time he visited, just before the duchess died, Errol had told him that it was his home.

"Wherever you are, if you ever feel like you need a place to stay, just come home. I'll be waiting for you and there's always room for you here."

David nodded to himself. He was going to Dorchester, even though he knew his friend was living in London with his family. He would have the place to himself and wondered if there were any servants left to take care of things. Definitely there must be. Even though the tide had turned for Errol and he was now living in one of the much sought after areas of London, David was sure he still made time to visit his estate.

Once he was settled, he would write and tell David that he was staying at the manor for a few days just to regain strength and when he was ready, would be leaving for the colonies.

No one welcomed her, no one invited her into their homes and no one gave her as much as a simple cup of water. It hurt Abby so much that everyone she had considered to be a friend had turned their backs on her. Guilt tore at her as she finally faced what Errol had been through just a few months ago.

"This is my punishment," she wept as she wandered aimlessly around the streets of London. She was so hungry and would have given anything just for a simple meal. She couldn't remember the last time she'd eaten, because she'd left home when the new owners came to take possession of the house. Truth be told, she had snuck away in the early hours of the morning. This was to escape the curious and mocking glances of those she knew would be waiting to witness her final humiliation. Being in a great hurry to get away, she hadn't even thought about taking any of her expensive gowns for then she would have sold them and got some money for her upkeep.

The nights were the worst and she'd found a small alcove at St. Thaddeus Church where she was christened as a baby and that was her temporary dwelling for two days. If bandits and wicked men didn't get her, the cold would certainly end her life. Abby couldn't believe that just a few days ago, she'd been sleeping in a most comfortable bed and with servants ready to do her every bidding. Now here she was, destitute, homeless and hungry and with no relief in sight.

She couldn't sleep at night because of the cold and fear of being attacked by someone. The hunger pangs almost drove her out of her mind but she was determined that she would find a way out of her current plight.

"Look out," someone shouted but it was too late and she felt darkness overcoming her even as she felt a searing pain on her side.

When Abby came to, she was lying on a soft bed and covered with warm blankets and there was a fire burning merrily in the grate. Where was she? Then she felt the presence of other people and turned her head slowly, only to encounter the last person she ever expected to see.

"How are you feeling?" Lillian asked their guest. "We're sorry about the accident."

"Accident?"

"Yes, my dear. You stepped right into the path of our carriage and our driver nearly ran you over. Mercifully, the wind flung you out of the way and we brought you home."

Of course, this was Errol's new home, actually it belonged to his nephews. She couldn't believe that life could be so cruel to her and she quickly closed her eyes, willing the tears not to fall.

"Are you in pain?" She felt a gentle hand on her forehead. "The doctor said you don't have any broken bones but will have aches and pains because of the bruising."

"Thank you," she said at last, humbled and deeply mortified to find herself indebted to the two people whose lives she'd set out to ruin just a few weeks ago. She couldn't help the tears and soon found herself sobbing as she said how sorry she was, over and over again.

"Abby, we don't hold anything against you," Errol told her when she had somewhat calmed down, and this brought a fresh bout of weeping.

"Hush now," Lillian was really concerned about their guest. When she'd been helping the maid to bathe her, she'd noticed how emaciated the poor girl was, as if she hadn't had a meal for days. "When you've had something to eat, things won't look so bleak."

5

A HOSTILE STRANGER

She was in Dorchester at the manor, a place she hadn't expected to ever return to. Yet this was going to be her home for the next few months as she sorted her life out. The beauty of it all was that it was quite secluded and apart from the old gardener and his wife who cleaned the house, the other servants were all in London taking care of their master.

Abby couldn't believe that Errol and Lillian had so kindly allowed her to use their home as a place of solace even after all she'd done to them. They had brushed her apologies aside, telling her not to worry about anything.

"It's a tough situation you are in right now, but things will get better somehow," Errol had told her. It was humbling to be their guest and be treated like a beloved sister, and not someone who had set out to ruin their lives. "Just take your time and sort your life out."

"You need a place that is out of the limelight so that you can have time to recuperate and also find refuge until all that is being said passes," Lillian told her. "Our home in Dorchester is there if you need it. Errol wants to tear down part of it and put up a better and sturdier structure but that won't be for another few months. We're waiting on an architect friend of his to return from Europe and then the renovations and restoration will begin. Meanwhile, you can stay there until you're ready to face the world again."

"How can I thank you for your kindness," she had wept as she held onto Lillian's hand. "I've never been so humiliated and rejected and it hurts terribly."

"I understand, but try not to dwell on your losses too much. You still have a good life ahead even though it doesn't seem like it right now. One day, you'll look back on this season of your life and realize that it is your turning point."

And indeed it was Abby's turning point. She'd spent hours seated at the window in the guest room just thinking about her future and past. Lillian had told her to be gentle with herself and forgive herself for making terrible mistakes. It was hard because she blamed herself for causing her father's death.

After a week of recuperating, she felt that she was ready to leave for Dorchester.

"Are you sure that you're ready to go now?"

"It's time that I grew up," she told Lillian, her smile was watery. "It has been a wakeup call for me and I remember my mama once telling me that wealth is fleeting and I should never place my trust in the things that I own." She shook her head. "I always thought Mama was strange because Papa was so wealthy," she choked on the words and cleared her throat. "My mother was a very simple woman. She had few gowns and the only things she had of value was the jewelery that my father gave her, which I lost," the pain tore at her heart. "How foolish I've been."

"You're only human and should be gentle and kind to yourself."

"I wish it was easy to just forget everything."

"You may never forget, but you will pass through and emerge on the other side," Lillian said. "Time has a way of healing our wounds and helping us accept our faults and mistakes. The secret, as my mother used to say, is to learn from every experience we go through and let it make us better people."

"You're so kind. My friends or those I thought were friends all turned their backs on me and wouldn't give me even a glass of water. Yet here you are even after I was so cruel to you. You and your husband opened the doors of your home to me, and have taken care of me. How will I ever repay your kindness?"

"Don't think about anything other than getting better and back on your feet. Errol told me to tell you that he will write you a letter to take to the village grocers so that if you need anything, they will provide and he will settle the accounts on a monthly basis."

It was mid afternoon when Abby entered Dorchester. She was in a covered carriage and though she could see people peering curiously at it as it passed, they couldn't see her. She couldn't bear their pitying looks and the shame that would follow when they saw and recognized her.

Old Paul Sims and his wife Rose were waiting for her and she realized that Errol must have sent them a message. They were one of the old servants who'd been with the family and she was surprised when they showed no contempt or disdain. Instead, they both had welcoming smiles on their faces as she got down from the carriage, which left a few minutes later.

"The master said you will be in the large guest room on the first floor. It's the best one since the others have already been stripped bare."

Abby had never lived in a house all alone, but she welcomed the solace. It would give her time to think and reflect on what she was going to do with her life. Now that she was here, she was determined not to be a burden to her hosts. They had no obligation at all to her, and she wasn't going to take advantage of their kindness. She would work for her living to prove to them that she was a changed woman now.

As she was settling down for a simple meal of bread, ham and warm milk, she heard the front door opening and thought it was Paul coming in. When she raised her eyes and encountered those of a stranger, her heart nearly stopped.

"Who are you, and what do you want?" She demanded, wishing Paul was close by but knowing that he was in his own cottage busy with his own chores. She'd told the couple that she could take care of herself and didn't need them waiting on her. The stranger looked frightening with his thick beard and fiery silverish eyes. "Who are you?"

"I should be asking the questions and not you," David said, placing his valise on the floor. "Who opened the door for you and what are you doing in Errol's house?"

"You know Errol?" Abby was surprised.

"We were at Eton together and he's my friend. Again I ask you, what are you doing here when just a few weeks ago, you were running your mouth off and scandalizing my friend?"

Abby looked down as her face flamed. He was just a stranger but he knew her story and she wished the ground would open up and swallow her. His gaze held contempt and she knew that she deserved it.

"Well," she raised her face. "Lillian is my friend and she allowed me to use their house until I get back on my feet again."

"Oh yes, I heard about your father, and I'm sorry for your loss."

Abby didn't know whether the stranger was mocking her or his condolences were sincere. She could never really tell these things because for so long, people had only spoken what she wanted to hear. No one had ever told her the truth about anything for fear of her wrath.

"Thank you."

"It was a really sad state of affairs, that man running off with your inheritance," he sat down and stretched his leg.

Abby put her hands over her ears, "Please just stop," tears welled in her eyes and she ran out of the room. David felt terrible at his callousness. It was just mean of him to attack her when she was so vulnerable. For her to have accepted help from Lillian and Errol meant that she was truly destitute! His friend was truly noble for giving refuge to Abby in her time of need, in spite of how things had ended between them.

With a sigh, he got to his feet and went in search of Abby. Her soft sobbing touched his heart even before he saw her as he entered the kitchen. She was leaning over the counter, wiping her eyes.

"I'm sorry, that was a mean thing for me to say. Please forgive me."

Abby didn't turn around but David's voice sounded sincere, so she nodded.

"My name is David Birch and as I told you, Errol and I were in school together. I spent most of my childhood here," he looked around the now cold kitchen. "It's always been home to me and I came here to recuperate. I didn't expect anyone else to be here, well apart from one or two servants since I know that Errol and his family now live in London most of the time."

6

FINDING COMMON GROUND

W hen David woke up the next day, it was nearly mid morning. He could hear the birds chirping cheerfully and downstairs, someone was singing softly. He lay back and listened but couldn't make out the words of the song. Still, it was a sweet voice and he closed his eyes and drifted off to sleep once again.

He woke up around noon and did some stretching as the doctor had told him to do, and was surprised to find a pitcher of warm water waiting at the washing stand. He quickly cleaned up and went downstairs, finding Abby just setting the table.

"I didn't know if you would be awake before evening," she said shyly. "I'd made you some breakfast and now lunch is also ready."

"Thank you," the surprise in his voice had her smiling. The mighty Lady Abigail Wentworth was now doing household chores.

"I somehow learnt how to cook even though I didn't like it." She twisted her lips wryly. "Never knew the skills would one day come in handy."

"There's always a first time for everything," he shrugged, happy to have someone waiting on him but also cautious enough not to be drawn in by Abby's beautiful smile. She really was a lovely woman, if only she had a heart to go with it.

Abby sensed David's withdrawal and turned back to return to the kitchen where she'd been making pancakes. She'd found a little flour and Rosie so graciously brought her a few eggs, but she would go out in search of work today, so that she would never have to depend on anyone.

"Thank you for making breakfast and lunch for me," David said when Abby brought in some more pancakes. She merely nodded and left the dining room. He had to be careful not to be drawn in by that alluring smile, for Lady Abigail Wentworth was trouble. He'd come here to recuperate and think about what he was going to do with the rest of his life. The last thing he needed was any kind of complication. It didn't occur to him that he was living in the large house with a woman, just the two of them. Society would frown on such living arrangements and declare that Abigail was ruined.

At that precise moment, that's what was running through Abby's mind. There was a scandal hovering over her head and if anyone was to find out that she was living in close proximity to a man who wasn't a relative, without a chaperone, there's no telling what else would be said about her. But she had nowhere to go and besides, the house was large enough for the two of them to avoid each other.

Abby was afraid of being judged because of her past and she knew that David was doing just that. It made her sad to know that she'd put good people through a lot of pain and humiliation, and yet they had opened their door for her when she needed help.

"I'll spend the rest of my life making restitution for my wicked ways," she murmured. The first thing she was going to do was to make sure that the house was in very good condition. Rosie had told her just that morning that she cleaned and dusted the house once a week because it would soon be torn down, at least most of it anyway.

"The master said we shouldn't bother too much with the place, but we have to earn our keep," Rosie had said. "My lady came and took away all the good items to the house in London. But when renovations are completed, those things will be returned."

"Whenever you need any help, please let me know."

"Yes, missy."

It was Rosie who directed her to the Armstrong family home. Though not nobility, they were wealthy gentry and according to the middle aged woman, the man was trying to buy himself a title. They had just bought a large manor that previously belonged to a baron who died without descendants and they needed all the help they could get.

"I would go myself but my back isn't what it used to be."

"Let me find out what kind of jobs they have to offer," Abby replied.

"Most likely scullery maid or something like that. But I would be careful," Rosie observed Abby with a critical eye. "Charles Armstrong, the lord of the manor, is said to have a roving eye and beauty such as yours is bound to be noticed. Just be careful, child."

"Thank you for the warning."

As Abby walked up the driveway to the large imposing house, she was praying that there would be a job for her, out of the path of trouble. The last thing she wanted was for anyone to find out who she was. The shame of going to work for others when all her life she'd enjoyed the services of servants was too much. But she had to prove to herself more than anything that she had changed. "And David too," a small voice said and she silenced it. What did she care what David Firth thought of her? She'd only known the man for two days and here she was already trying to seek his approval.

Taking Rosie's advice, she'd donned an old bonnet that the former found for her among her clothes. Then she deliberately smudged her face with a little soot to hide the milky white skin. "You'll do," had been the best words she'd heard in a while, when Rosie nodded her approval. "Now you look like an ordinary scullery maid."

"But I am a servant."

Rosie shook her head. "I know nobility when I see it and you are no ordinary chit. I remember that you used to come by the estate when Lord Errol was here. Something must have happened to change your lot in life, but you're a noble woman through and through. Your clothes may not say it, but your bearing and speaking do so. Still, no matter what happens, never lose what you have inside."

There were a few other young ladies waiting in the courtyard at the back, obviously here for the job. When Mrs. Melinda Armstrong as she introduced herself came out, she looked at them all critically. "I might as well take you all in," she said haughtily. "You look like you need the work and this large house needs cleaning from top to bottom."

Abby was relieved when she was put to work in the kitchen, scrubbing pots and pans. But her relief was short lived because the cook was a nasty piece of work. She demanded to be addressed as Madam Hattie and was very free with her slaps and using a ladle to rap someone's knuckles. Because she wasn't used to the work, Abby's hands were aching by the time evening came around and she was allowed to leave. She was subjected to further humility when her body was frisked thoroughly by the cook. She had rough calloused hands and it took Abby great effort not to show her revulsion at being treated thus.

"Can't be too careful with you village girls," Hattie said. "You love stealing the silver and I'm the one who will have to bear the brunt of it all should anything go missing. And no carrying any leftover food." She took away the old apple that Abby had put in her apron pocket which she had intended to eat as she walked back home. It hurt to see Hattie dump the apple into the waste basket. "Go on now, and be here before light to start work tomorrow."

7

FACING REALITY

D avid couldn't believe that he missed Abby. He paced through the house restlessly, wondering what was happening to him. He'd come out here to recuperate but he was more tense than ever before and it was all because of the young woman who shared the house with him.

He hadn't seen her in days and when he'd asked Rosie, had been informed that she went out in search of work so she could earn some money. It was hard to imagine Abigail being anyone's servant and his heart was filled with so much compassion for her. This woman had been through a lot and she was trying to pick up the pieces of her life. But for how long would she work as a servant? This wasn't her lot and he longed to find her and tell her that with her education she could be a governess.

One evening as he was strolling through the garden, he heard the sound of someone weeping. He frowned when he recognized it to be Abby. The sound was coming from a part of the garden that was poorly lit by an old lantern.

"Lady Abigail, what's wrong? Has someone offended you?"

"Don't call me that," she cried out bitterly and he saw in the dim light that her face was smudged with soot. "Don't ever call me lady again."

"My lady, setbacks can never change who you are," he sat down on the slab beside her. "I'm sorry that you're so sad."

"I deserve this," Abby wiped her tears but more took their place. "This is my punishment for how I was before." David wanted to protest that it wasn't so but wisely held his peace. "All though, I lived a privileged life, never caring how other people lived and what pain they were going through. I took servants in my father's household for granted and never once treated them like human beings." She put her face in her hands and wept. David let her cry so she could relieve the pain in her heart. She raised her face, even though it was getting dark and he couldn't see her very well. "Until the day that my father died and I lost everything, I didn't bother learning any of the servants' names and never allowed them to look at me in the face."

David didn't know what to say. His own sister-in-law behaved in exactly the same way as Abby was describing. Servants were treated as part of the furniture and fixtures, never being acknowledged at all. It was a wakeup call for even him, and he wished he had paid more attention to the men and women who had served his family for years.

"Now that I'm a maid, I know how it feels. No one cares whether I live or die, no one cares when the fire burns me or I'm scalded by hot liquids in the kitchen," she shook her head. "My knees have hardened, my hands have blisters and my knuckles are raw from all the scrubbing and cleaning of pots and pans. Yet no one even cares."

"I'm really sorry to hear that."

"Don't be. This is my penance. Now I understand why my mother used to tell me never to trust in riches and wealth. These things aren't permanent and people's stations in life change. Take the Armstrong family who I'm working for as an example. They're new money simply because Mr. Armstrong happened to be in the right place at the right time. He went to India as a soldier of the East India Company to guard the British interests abroad. One evening as he and one of his senior officers were strolling in the garden, they came across a cobra," she shuddered. "What struck them about this particular serpent was that it seemed to be lying on glowing stones. They wanted to kill it but one of the Indian servants told them it was a god of some sort, and promised to show them more glowing stones if only they would spare the life of the serpent."

David's interest was piqued. "Did he?"

"Yes. The man led them to a sort of cave where they had to jump over a few serpents before they reached the rubies. The two men had found one of the richest deposits of rubies in Madikeri, in south western India. Of course the company took most of the rubies but allowed the two gentlemen to keep some."

"You've learnt a lot in the short time you've been in the household."

That garnered a smile from Abby. "Mama used to say servants have ears but we never thought it was true. Even though we're treated like wallpaper, there's so much one can learn by listening in on the masters' conversation."

David reached out a hand in the dark and touched Abby's arm. "You impress me greatly, my lady."

"Why?"

"Apart from the earlier outburst, you seem to have taken a bad situation and turned it into an educational one. Go on with the story of the Armstrongs."

"Well, Mr. Armstrong decided that being a soldier wasn't enough so he found a way of investing in exporting silks, spices and indigo dye to England and other parts of Europe. Now the man, once a mere foot soldier is wealthy beyond words and looking for a title to purchase."

What pleased David was that Abby's voice was devoid of envy. She was merely telling a story about the family she worked for and he realized that she was really a changed woman.

"Life is very strange," he said at last. "I've seen combat while in France fighting Napoleon and something small can change a person's whole life," he absentmindedly rubbed his injured leg. "I woke up one morning, full of health and by evening, I had nearly lost my life."

"Never will I ever take people for granted again," the sadness was back in her voice and David wanted to reach out and hold her. "Look at me now," she sniffed. "I had over ten offers of marriage and scoffed at the men who presented themselves, thinking my life was better than theirs and that I deserved better." She gave a small sob. "Now look at me, no man will ever want me because I'm nothing more than a common scullery maid."

"Abigail, please don't degrade yourself so."

"It's the truth and much as it hurts, I deserve it all."

"It's not true."

"What do you mean? Are you blind?"

"I meant it's not true that no man will want you," he paused to let his words sink in.

"Oh!"

"Yes, Abby," he finally took her hands in the dark. "I've been in love with you since we met but you're a lady, the daughter of a baron" she snorted softly but he ignored the sound. "You're royalty and though you may be down for now, some day you will rise again. You're determined and that makes me humble." He sighed. "I came to Dorchester to hide from the world after my injuries and also to plan my next course of action. There I was, feeling sorry for myself and yet it was always obvious from the beginning that I would never amount to much. Being a second son isn't really a blessing, and if my father hadn't bought me a commission in the army, only God knows where I would be right now."

"Your speech and manner speaks of nobility too."

"Well, you might as well know it now. My father was the Duke of Somerset and my brother Edward is now the duke. But I can't be at home because I'm only a second son."

"England is a beautiful country but some of the laws need to be changed."

"Not in a hundred years," he smiled at the indignation in her voice. "Still, we're better than so many around the world."

"You could be right."

"You're making me lose track of what I was trying to tell you, my lady."

Abby giggled softly and the sound warmed David's heart. "You're one of the most beautiful women England has ever produced and believe me, in just a few months' time you will have sorted your life out. The scandal will be over and people will be more receptive towards you. I wouldn't be surprised if the Regent Prince sends for you in order to make a good match for you. Our Regent is a man with a good eye, and he knows value when he sees it. It's just a matter of time."

"Why are you telling me all this?"

"Because I want you to know that I love you, but I have nothing. My commission in the army is over due to my injury, I have nothing to my name and right now, here I am seeking refuge in the home of a dear friend. All I have is a small army pension which isn't enough to take care of my own needs. What's more, I'm lame and broke and with no prospects for the future. In times past, I would be burnt at the stake for even daring to speak with such a noble woman as yourself."

She giggled again.

"I hope I haven't offended you, my lady."

"You haven't," Abby wanted to jump up and dance. This was a handsome man who had just declared that he loved her. He had nothing but she knew that for the first time in her life, she was in love.

"What are you saying, my lady?"

"You really are blind," she smiled. "I've been avoiding you because I know you think I'm just a flighty woman who caused a lot of problems for your friend."

"At first that's what I thought, but now that I've seen you working so hard these past few weeks, I believe you're a true noble woman not just by birth, but at heart too."

"You say such nice things."

"But true, nevertheless. Do I stand a chance with you, my fair lady?"

"Yes," she whispered and David gave a shout of joy.

8

SIMPLE THINGS IN LIFE

Abby smiled when she looked at the small bouquet of wild pansies that Rosie had picked for her just that morning. This was a far cry from her previous wedding arrangements but she was so happy that she didn't care that she was getting married in Rosie's old wedding gown that had been adjusted by the two of them so it would fit her slender frame.

Their witnesses were the middle aged couple who beamed with pleasure at having such an honour bestowed upon them.

"Mark my words, my dear husband. These two are fine nobles even though they don't look like it," Rosie had remarked to Paul just that morning. "One day, it will be said that you and I stood up for two nobles, common folk like us."

"You're a very romantic woman and I love you for that," Paul kissed his wife's cheek. "But face reality, what nobility lives like two paupers? They scrounge for whatever little they can get."

"It was before your time and mine, but I heard David telling Abby that he used to come here to visit the master when they were younger. I seem to remember something about an engagement between Miss Abby and our master but I could be wrong," she shrugged. "My memory fails me but there's something about these two that tells me they're no ordinary folk like you and me. Mark my words."

Even as the local vicar was conducting their simple but deeply moving wedding ceremony, Abby and David only had eyes for each other. Reverend Peter Smith was happy to perform the wedding of two people who were clearly so much in love. This love, he thought, was bound to last forever. He'd wed many couples in the past and many of them weren't even in love. Some didn't even like each other. All they did was have lavish ceremonies filled with pomp and glory all to prove their worth in money. A few months and sometimes even weeks later, he would receive news of course in the form of rumours, that the couple were now living in sin with other people.

But not these two. They were as poor as could be for they could barely afford the certificate of marriage that he was to give them, and yet the love they felt for each other could be felt within the walls of the small church. If only more couples waited to fall in love, the real and pure kind, not merely lust or for other selfish reasons, then marriages would be heaven on earth as the good Lord intended from the beginning.

"I wish I could have provided a carriage to take you home, my love," David's eyes were filled with regret when they stepped out of the church. The elderly couple had already left for home because Rosie had promised to make them a wedding lunch.

"My darling," Abby turned to him and touched his cheek gently. "We have each other and that's all that matters. This is our day and what's important is the love we share."

"You're such a beautiful woman both inside and outside, and I know that you will bring me a lot of goodness." He took her hand. "I don't want you to go and work for those people. We'll make do with what we have until something better comes up."

"Thank you for saying that for I really had no heart to return. Mr. Armstrong is a very peculiar fellow and makes me very uncomfortable."

They held hands and walked home slowly, just enjoying each other's company and their love. Abby thought about the past and how different things were right now. She would never in a million years have imagined herself walking on foot and holding hands with the man who had just become her husband. The ring David had given her was one he had bought at the village square just the previous day. It was cheap and as she looked at it, laughing softly.

"What's making my beautiful bride so happy?"

"I was just thinking of how the Lord can change a person. It seems as if I'm in a dream right now. Never would I have imagined myself enjoying the simple things of life like fresh air, wild flowers and this ring. It just feels so right, somehow."

"You deserve more and better and when our lot changes, I will give you everything your heart desires."

Abby smiled, quite contented with her life at that moment. "All that matters is being with you for the rest of my life and knowing that you love me."

"There's no doubt about that," he stopped when they got to the gate. "That's strange, were we expecting any guests?"

"That's Lord and Lady Campbell's carriage. I remember it because it nearly ran me over some weeks ago."

David didn't know how his friend would react when he found out that he had married Abby. "I hope there isn't any trouble."

"Why?"

"You and I being married is rather odd."

"Well, the deed's done and so let's just find out what happens next."

The duke and duchess were genuinely happy to see the two. "I know Rosie stole your moment but that woman can never keep a secret," Errol smiled at his two friends. "We hear congratulations are in order."

"Yes, your grace," David bowed as Abby curtsied.

"Please remember that we're peers," Errol said, shaking David's hand and kissing Abby's cheek. Lilly hugged both of them. "My duchess and I are so happy for the two of you. It's about time you had some goodness in your lives for a change."

"You're welcome to share our simple wedding lunch," Abby said shyly. She couldn't believe that just a few months ago she was engaged to Errol and broke it off because she was really jealous of his little innocent nephews. She felt a twinge or remorse and it must have shown on her face, for Lilly pulled her aside.

"Shall we go to the kitchen for a word," the latter said.

"Yes, my lady."

"Abby, you're my peer so please no titles. How have you been?"

"Really happy," she said simply and Lilly nodded.

"You look so happy and contented. Errol tells me David is a good man and he'll take very good care of you."

"So you knew he was staying here?"

"No, we just found out when we arrived. It was Rosie who told us that the two of you arrived on the same day. As we waited for you to return from church, Errol told me about David and how they spent most of their school holidays together. David has always been a loner, being the second son with no prospects. His happiest days were those spent here in Dorchester, no wonder that he returned here when he needed somewhere to go."

"He doesn't talk much about his family."

"I know only a little of what Errol told me." They entered the kitchen. "We have some news for you, but I'll let the duke convey it."

"Didn't you come with the boys?"

"The journey is cumbersome and they had slight colds. In any case, we're going back right away so it would have been a waste of time to bring them. Those two are just too boisterous."

Abby felt something like envy when she heard the pride in Lilly's voice, but quickly quashed it. But for her selfishness, she might have been the boys' mother.

"Do you regret not marrying Errol?" Lilly asked in a quiet voice.

Abby tilted her head to one side and then shook it slowly. "A few weeks ago, I might have said yes. But now I see that all things were working for my good. With Errol, it would have been a marriage of convenience only. He needed my dowry and I needed a handsome man to show off to the world," she laughed in self-derision. "But now, I know that I married David because I love him and he loves me too. We both have nothing but we're so happy together. I know that somehow, things will work out for us."

To her surprise, Lilly reached out and hugged her. "All will be well, you'll see."

And Errol repeated the same words to them as they finished their simple meal of freshly baked bread, smoked ham and warm milk. Rosie had baked a fruit cake to commemorate the wedding and though simple, it was one of the most wholesome meals Abby had ever eaten.

"After you left, Abby, I got in touch with a friend of mine who is a Bow Street Runner. He did some investigations and I'm pleased to let you know that the Frenchman who conned you was arrested in Paris. Apparently, he tried to do the same thing to another woman but she was smarter and her brothers were alert. The French law enforcers are working with their British counterparts to try and salvage anything for you and others who lost their wealth and precious items to that man."

Abby's face was red with embarrassment and David reached out a hand and touched her arm. "It's all well, my love," he said softly and she nodded slightly.

"The British Foreign office has taken the matter up and immediately when anything comes up, I will let you know."

"Thank you so much," Abby said. "You really didn't have to and I have learnt to live without what I lost."

"Still, there's hope that things will turn out better for you."

"We just have one request," David didn't want his beloved to continue feeling slighted.

"Go ahead," Errol urged.

"We need your permission to continue living here for a short while as we think of what to do next. I've been thinking about applying to the Foreign office so I can be posted in the colonies and Abby is fine with the idea."

"Take all the time you need because we won't be using the manor for a while. We're in the process of carrying out some renovations but we're not in a hurry. Lord and Lady Worthington left the town house for their sons and we're also renovating their country home in Exeter, the one that got burnt. The boys will need their homes when they grow up, so once we're done with those, we can then concentrate on our own."

"We're most grateful to you, my lord and lady."

9

RESTORATION

A bby woke up early the next morning but found that her husband wasn't in the bedroom with her. Thinking that he had perhaps returned to the one he'd been using, she started getting out of bed to go in search of him when the door opened.

"What are you doing out of bed this early?" David exclaimed, hurrying to the bed. "I just went to check on Rosie who had promised to bring us some milk."

"When I didn't find you, I thought you'd gone back to your old room."

"Why would I do that?" He chuckled when her face turned red. "In any case, we had an early morning visitor and I really don't know what to make of it all."

"I didn't hear anyone coming in."

"That's because you were sound asleep when I left the room. But in short, the messenger or should I say messengers are from Somerset, my county seat."

"Is everything alright?"

David shook his head and then she saw the sadness in his eyes. "My brother, the duke is dead."

"I'm so sorry, my darling," she took his hand. "I'm very sorry for your loss."

"My brother and I weren't as close as we should have been and it breaks my heart that he died all alone, sad and full of despair."

Abby frowned slightly. "Didn't you tell me he was married?"

"He was," David shook his head. "It was my sister-in-law who caused his sudden collapse and subsequent death."

"I don't understand."

"From what my men tell me, Camille loved to throw parties and spend lavishly. Mercifully, my father had tied up his wealth so she couldn't access it all at one time, else we would be talking about a different matter altogether. What happened is that apparently one of the men who frequented the estate was her lover. A few days ago, Camille took a good amount of my brother's money and ran away with her lover. The last they were heard of, they were headed to Europe. Edward loved Camille so much, and I guess the shock caused him to have a seizure and by the time the doctor was called, he was already dead."

"Oh dear," Abby couldn't imagine the shock the man must have received. "Did she make away with all his wealth?"

"No. As I said, my father had tied up all his assets in such a way that Edward was to continue receiving an allowance until he turned thirty, then he would become responsible for the whole estate. I believe our father thought that by that time they would have children and be more accountable. My poor brother was only twenty seven."

"It's really sad."

"Now I have to return to Somerset and take the title since I'm next in line." David looked at Abby and she saw the uncertainty in his eyes. "I don't know if I have it in me to be a duke."

"You're strong, brave and care about people. Those are qualities that are important, and besides, I think an estate such as yours has a good manager who will guide you."

"My wise bride," he kissed her forehead. "You were destined to be a duchess."

"I didn't marry you for your title."

"No you didn't, for you married me when I had nothing. Yet now we are going to take up our rightful position. Didn't I tell you that things will one day change for you?"

"Indeed you did."

For many years thereafter, everyone said Somerset had never had such a lovely and wonderful duchess who genuinely cared about her subjects. Many didn't know the full story of Lady Abigail Wentworth's previous life and those who did really didn't care.

The duke and duchess were one of the happiest and loving couples that the county had seen and their estate flourished as did their people.

TO DELIGHT A DUKE

1
DISCONTENTED LADY

Poverty hurt and Antoinette Martineau often said if it had a face and a body, she would have done all she could to challenge it to a duel and come out the better of the two. From when she was a child, she hadn't understood why people treated her and her mother with scorn and disdain.

It was only when she turned eighteen that the truth finally emerged. She didn't belong in Charente, Normandy and neither did her mother. She was the daughter of a man who was so despised by his own family that even saying his name was taboo.

Emile Martineau was a smooth talker who had squandered all his family's wealth including selling off most of the land, leaving them nearly destitute. When he ran away to make his fortune in Paris, the whole village was pleased to see him go. But a few months later, Emile had returned with an English girl, Hilda Cummings. She was pregnant at the time and immediately after Antoinette was born, her father disappeared, never to be seen or heard from again.

Her mother had confessed on her death bed three years ago that even though her life had been hard, she was glad to have kept the child. "You're the only good thing that came out of my union with that man," Hilda had said tearfully, her voice filled with regret. "I had a good job as a lady's maid and the woman I worked for really trusted me, but I broke her heart and betrayed her."

"How Mama?"

"Emile seduced me and convinced me to take my lady's jewelery and money and we eloped. He deceived me that he was a titled nobleman, a count, which is equivalent to an earl in England. I was young and foolish and succumbed to his seduction. When we got here, my eyes were finally opened but it was too late. He had squandered all the money I had stolen and besides that, I was with child. His family never accepted me for they believed I was one of the women on whom Emile squandered his family's wealth."

"But why did you stay, Mama?"

"Where else was I to go?"

"Back to England."

"I would have been arrested and then also, the shame I had brought upon my family wouldn't allow me to return. I made my bed and have spent the past eighteen years lying on it. I just don't want you to continue suffering when I'm gone."

"Mama, you can't leave me alone."

"My dear child," Hilda gently stroked her daughter's hair. "I've been ailing for a while but didn't want you to know. You were still very young and I prayed that I would be allowed to see you grow into a young woman before I was taken away. God has been gracious and I can't ask for any more. Please promise me that you will go back to England and find my people. Tell them that I died repenting of my sins and waywardness."

Her mother had died a few days later and it took Antoine three years to come to terms with her death. Thankfully, her mother had taught her English and she spoke it fluently, which made it easy for her to find work as a tutor. She actually took over her mother's old post and for three years she'd been able to earn a decent living. But things were quickly getting out of hand because the young boys she'd previously tutored were now grown up and began making lewd suggestions to her.

Perhaps it was time to go back to England and find her mother's family. She wasn't sure what the reception would be like but she would at least try. Speaking English gave her an advantage for she would find work as a

French tutor. She spoke both languages fluently and it would also be a chance for her to make a better life for herself.

As she was preparing for her journey to England, she received a message from Paris that her father was dead. This came in the form of an old trunk that was delivered to his family home but the messenger was turned away and redirected to the dilapidated house she'd lived in with her mother and a few other boarders who mostly minded their own business. The presence of the three or so elderly people gave her a sense of security.

The only thing the messenger could tell her was that her father had died while in prison and she didn't know whether to mourn or feel relieved. For so long, she'd feared that her father would return and she would have to face him. She felt nothing but hatred for the man who had deceived her poor mother, brought her to Normandy, a long way from home and abandoned her to her own fate.

"Relief at least," she murmured as she opened the trunk and wriggled her nose at the musty smell coming from within. It was obvious that anything of importance had been looted and it was a wonder that the trunk had even found its way back to Emile Martineau's home county. Someone must have had at least some respect for him. At first all Antoine could see were old clothes and papers that looked useless. She wanted to burn them but decided to hold on to them for a day or two as she decided what to do with the trunk and its contents. It was a reminder of the father she'd never seen but whose memory left a bitter taste in her mouth.

Her mother's tale of woe had made her wary of men and any kind of entanglement with them thus she didn't realize that her disinterest added to her allure. Men were interested in her but she didn't give them a chance to get close.

"Never give in to the wiles of the French," her mother would tell her time and time again. "They will only use you and then abandon you when you're in trouble."

There were of course, a few good men but Antoine didn't think her mother would have approved, for Hilda had come to despise everything French. Even though she was half French, Antoine always felt that she was more English because she'd taken her mother's fair complexion, blond hair and blue eyes. She'd seen how badly her mother had been treated by her father's people and didn't think she ever wanted to go through that in her life. Once was enough, thank you!

Lord Richard Foxworth, the Duke of Hampshire was in a foul mood and his servants knew to keep their distance. It wasn't often that Richard lost his temper but when he did, it was often accompanied by a few broken items in the house. The only person who had the ability to calm him down when he was in one of his rare rages, was the

Dowager Duchess, Lady Amelia his mother. But she was visiting friends in the countryside when the solicitor brought him the news that had him in a rage.

"That French man," he hissed through his teeth, wishing he could find the culprit who had put his whole estate in jeopardy. Not only had Emile Martineau caused his beloved aunt's death, for Richard blamed the man solely, but he had also made off with the family's precious items. The most important of all was the signet ring which if it fell in the wrong hands, could cause him to lose everything.

His mother and Aunt Edith had never gotten along and when the latter fell into the clutches of the unscrupulous French man, the former had felt quite justified. "I always said your father's sister was a scatterbrain but you thought I was being unkind to her," Lady Amelia didn't gloat, but there was satisfaction in her voice. "Which person in their senses takes the family jewelery and hands it over to a total stranger? What your grandmother didn't give me went to your aunt. In her foolishness she just handed everything over to the man on a silver platter. " She turned angry eyes towards her sister-in-law. "Are you sure you didn't give your lover the house too?"

"Ma, you know that Aunt Edith was in love with that fellow," Richard defended his aunt strongly. "I don't think there's anything to worry about. We can always replace the jewels if we want, but they belonged to Aunt Edith."

"She's here, let her speak for herself and tell us how we're going to solve this issue," Lady Amelia had goaded her sister-in-law. "Is there anything else we should know about?" But Edith was too distraught to even say a word. She pinned away until one morning they found her dead in her bed. At first everyone thought she had taken some poison but the coroner ruled that out.

"This poor woman died of a broken heart," he pronounced and Lady Amelia had scoffed.

"There's no such thing as dying from a broken heart," she insisted. "Edith was just a weak person who rather than face what she'd done, chose the easy way out. That Frenchman must be pursued so he can pay for his crimes."

"Ma, please don't say that," Richard had begged. "The man is long gone and where would we even begin?"

"You better be sure that we didn't lose much more of value tham Edith's jewelery. Somehow I never trusted your aunt so make sure you found out everything she may have given that wicked man."

Richard had strongly rebuked his mother for her insensitivity and Lady Amelia had thereafter kept her thoughts to herself. But now almost a year later, Richard wished he had pursued the lost items like his mother had insisted. At the time he'd felt sorry for his aunt and didn't want her to feel any worse. Now, he had just found out that the family signet ring was missing. How hadn't he notice that before, he wondered. Had he been too sympathetic and blinded by the love he had for his paternal aunt that he'd subconsciously overlooked many things?

He might have carried on in his ignorance if the family solicitor hadn't come and alerted him to the fact that something was wrong.

"Mr. Maynard, I'm telling you that I had no idea that the signet ring was missing," he looked at the man who sat across from him. "You know that for this past year, I left all business decisions for you to handle so there was no time I used that ring to seal any documents."

Lawrence Maynard had served Richard's father, who'd been a very shrewd and meticulous man, unlike the son who seemed to have his head in the clouds. But he wisely kept his thoughts to himself for fear of receiving a tongue lashing. Still, he wished Lady Amelia was present for then he would have had the courage to speak his mind freely. The dowager loved her son but not to the extent that she overlooked his faults.

"I'm afraid the family seal has been used for some questionable transactions and vast withdrawals were made from your family trust."

"What?" Richard sat upright, hitting the surface of the desk with his open hand. "How did that happen?"

"Mercifully, your father had given instructions that when the sums reached a certain limit, your mother was to be consulted in the event that he wasn't around. We only noticed the anomalies when the bank contacted us for instructions to transfer a large sum of money to a French bank."

"I don't believe that for a full year we've been losing money and you knew nothing of it," Richard glared at his solicitor but Lawrence was undaunted. He knew the young man was only trying to cover up his own inadequacies, but still wished the duchess had been around. She would have put the young man in his place.

"Your grace, it's a good thing we noticed this but you have to move fast and find that signet ring before the culprit sells the house from under your feet."

Richard waited until Lawrence had left before he gave full vent to his anger. One of his mother's precious vases was the victim and he rang the bell impatiently. A young lad came trembling into the study.

"See to that mess," he told him, before picking up his cane and striding out of the study.

"Yes, your grace."

2

SHOCKING DISCOVERY

ay 20th 18..

"**M** *The foolish woman thinks I'll marry her. These English women are simpletons and it would be something akin to a curse for me to marry another of them. Good thing I married the other one so I have an excuse not to fall into that trap again.*

Lady Eugenia Craydon is my latest conquest. She believes that if she leaves her husband, I will be forced to marry her. Poor foolish and delusional broad. All I needed were the jewels that she wears so proudly. And now that I have them in my possession, I can control her as I wish.

This is such an easy game that it grows boring. Can't I find a worthy opponent to deal with?"

Antoine felt revulsion growing within her as she read her father's journal. There were entries dating back years as she read about how he'd seduced young unmarried ladies and even married ones, just to get their money and other precious items. It was humiliating to think that she was born of such a one as this. He was callous and didn't seem in the least bit ashamed of what he'd done.

The two most recent entries, were nearly six months ago and she knew it had all stopped when her father was arrested and put in prison. A befitting place for him, no doubt since he had committed a lot of evils against unsuspecting women.

"July 13th 18....

Lady Edith Foxworth, a spinster who imagines that she and I can become man and wife. What a farce!! The woman is an old maid and seducing her had its benefits. Gullible and desperate she was like a ripe apple just waiting to fall into my hands.

Do I feel guilty at all? No. These women deserve everything that is coming to them because of their weaknesses. I need the money, they need the attention. It's a fair trade and I shouldn't be judged for my actions."

Antoine turned another page.

"November 20th, 18....

Perhaps this little miss came closest to trapping me into marriage. It was a narrow escape, and I had to flee England for she pasted my photos all over the papers to show proof of that stupid engagement. Took me by surprise, that one. Little Lady Abigail Wentworth. This one was a most worthy opponent for she never gave in. I feel something akin to respect for her, no wonder she nearly had me trapped. Still, I came out the victor when I walked away with everything she and her arrogant father own.

I am the master and everyone should acknowledge that."

Her father was a narcissist who loved himself and felt like he was entitled to gaining from others in whatever way he wished. He'd turned respectable women into tools of his mockery and spite and the fact that he showed no remorse whatsoever, shocked her beyond anything. How could a human being be so vile and wicked, she wondered.

She couldn't imagine that she was his offspring and regretted she had insisted on keeping the family name. Her mother had wanted her to use her maiden name but she'd resisted, taking pride in being half French and half English. Now she was sorry for everyone knew her as Antoine Martineau, the daughter of a scoundrel.

Thankfully, the family name was fairly common in South France and she could lay claim to being a descendant of another clan. But deep within her, she would always know that she was the daughter of a man who had used, misused and abused women in the worst way possible, then betrayed them.

There were a few last pages and she forced herself to read them.

"No one will ever find out where I keep my trophies. It's very regrettable that circumstances and need forced me to sell a few of those precious pieces in order to survive and maintain my lifestyle. But who will ever know that my wealth lies buried in the vault that I prepared for my inevitable demise? I will be buried with everything I have acquired, for I shall most certainly need my wealth in the afterlife. The Lady of The Torch bears my great secret, and no other.

How like a prince I shall lie, on a bed of the most precious jewels and gems. A befitting send off for a worthy noble such as myself."

Antoine shook her head in wonder. Her father had been completely demented and if what she suspected was true, a real mad man. All she had to do was find the vault that he had purchased and prepared, no doubt by using the money from the precious items he'd stolen and sold.

Just who was the Lady of the Torch, Antoine wondered. Was this her father's mistress in Paris, perhaps the only woman he'd ever loved? She tried to put the journal away but found herself returning to it and the more she read, the more she discovered her father's secret. When she'd first read it, she wondered what the small numbers at the bottom of each page were, then she began to suspect that they were the sum of items that he'd taken from each woman.

That meant that her father had a great stash somewhere, no doubt being guarded for him by the Lady of the Torch.

Would this lady, whoever she was, be willing to hand over the stolen items so she could return them to their rightful owners?

That was going to be her mission from now on. To find and restore whatever her father had taken away by devious means. Poor women, she thought. What a fiend her father had been but she would blot out the blight against her lineage by restoring and making restitution wherever possible.

It took Antoine nearly five days before she discovered that the Lady of the Torch was an old chapel which hadn't been used since the French Revolution. It was still under the Catholic Church but a bigger and more modern chapel had been built a few metres away from it.

She found out quite by accident as she was waiting for a carriage to take her to yet another part of Paris. She'd sold everything of value to make this journey and hoped her money wouldn't run out before she set things right back in England. Her father's journal had specified five names whose jewels he had acquired. The rest, he'd said were cheap trinkets that had funded his lifestyle. The more precious ones were his trophies.

As she was waiting for the carriage, she overheard an elderly woman mentioning the Lady of the Torch and she subtly drew near, only to discover that the woman wanted to visit her husband's grave at that location. Excited because her quest was nearly over, Antoine had purchased a ticket to the place and alighted after the old lady and her companion.

There was a gardener who tended the few graves but she could also see elaborate tombs and vaults.

"Excuse me, sir," she approached him and he raised himself up. He looked like he'd lived forever, because his hair was very white against his grizzled skin. "I'm looking for my family's vault, reserved by my father."

"The name please."

"Emile Martineau," she said and held her breath.

"Fine young man," the gardener said. "He was here a few months ago to bury his young son. Very sad and moving ceremony and I could see how sad he felt."

"Yes, we lost my brother," Antoine put a handkerchief to her eyes, praying that the man wouldn't ask for details. "I'd like to visit the vault please."

"This way," the man was tall and walked with a stoop. Antoine's heart was pounding loudly and she feared that the man might hear. "Each family has their own key, did you bring one?"

"Yes, sir." And Antoine was grateful for getting her father's useless trunk back and for whoever had packed it hurriedly. They hadn't bothered to read the journal or they would have found the single key at the bottom of the trunk and been here on this quest.

"Good. Take your time for I like to say death is peaceful." The man frowned. "I haven't seen your father in a while. Is he alright?"

"He traveled to Charente, our family home."

"I see." He took her to the back of the small chapel which though very old, had been well maintained. He opened a side door which led into an empty room. It housed a number of vaults. "Many people don't like being here all alone and ask me to sit with them. Will you be afraid?"

"The dead can do no harm to us, it's the living that we should fear most," Antoine quoted her mother. "I've just come to pay my respects to my brother and then I will be leaving again."

"Take all the time you need for he's going nowhere. If the casket is too heavy to open, I can help you. It's the third from the other end."

"Should I need your help, I will come and find you," she promised.

Antoine waited until the man had left before taking a deep breath and walking towards the vault he had indicated. It bore her family name and she put the key in and turned. There was a single well polished white casket which she knew contained no body and she furtively raised it. She nearly dropped the lid when she saw the collection of jewelery. They sparked as if to mock her and she lowered the lid once again, wondering how she was going to carry it all out without being spotted or raising anyone's suspicion. It wasn't much but she was sure they were heavy and all she had was a canvas bag.

She opened the casket once again and stuffed as much as she could into the bag she had, glad to note that she had taken nearly half. But the bag was heavy and she was going to have to find a way of walking without trouble. An idea suddenly came to her and she spread the jewelery and then tied the bag around her middle, glad that she'd worn a large cloak. If anyone cared to observe her closely, they would think she was with child and she prayed no one would draw closer.

It took her two days to empty the vault and when she was in her small boarding room which she'd taken in mid town Paris, she looked at the items and prayed that God would protect her. "I'm returning them to the owners so please don't allow me to fall into the wrong hands," she pleaded. "I'm only doing what my father should have done, had he come to his senses. The owners of these items need them, please help me across the channel and into England without being discovered."

She remembered what her mother had told her one time. *"From time immemorial, women have learnt how to hide things on their selves. For example, during times of war, many ladies sewed their jewels into the seams of their dresses and passed through perilous places undetected. That was how I managed to get my lady's jewelery out of the house without anyone being the wiser."*

For the next two days, Antoine was kept busy sewing different items of jewelery into her garments, careful to place them in such a way so no one would be suspicious. It was as she was putting the last pieces in that she came across the ring and stared at it in horror. It was a family signet ring, no doubt belonging to an important family. Of all the items, she deduced that this was the most precious and felt the urgency of restoring it back to the rightful owners.

Her mother had served a noble woman and once told her that the family signet ring was valued above all their other jewels for it was a representation of the family. *"When a family needed to prove and authenticate any documents, they would seal them with the ring. Lost jewels and clothes can easily be replaced, but not a ring. It is a very special heirloom and guarded with a lot of care."*

Yet she held one in her hand and she strained to see the inscription on the inside of the back. Without a magnifying glass, she could only make out the name Fox but was sure that once she got to England, someone would recognize the seal and lead her to the owner.

3
CATCH THE THIEF

"You say your aunt lost the family signet ring?"

"Yes, Ma," Richard was sweating even though he tried not to show it. His mother was being too calm and he knew that always happened before she reacted. "It was one of the items that Aunt Edith gave that Frenchman."

"What aren't you telling me?" Lady Amelia peered at her son through narrowed blue eyes, like his own. "What are you hiding from me?"

"Ma, I'm really sorry that I should have been more observant but wasn't." He took a deep breath. Might as well get it all out and face the consequences. "Mr. Maynard informed me that someone used it to withdraw large sums of money from the family trust. It was only spotted when the person tried to transfer a huge sum to a bank in Paris."

"That wicked Frenchman, no doubt."

"I think so. But after my investigations, I was informed that he died in prison about six months ago and this request for transfer was made a few days ago. Someone else, maybe an accomplice must have tried to get the money."

"Or else, he'd made a payment or IOU to someone who decided to cash it in after his death."

Richard was surprised at his mother's astuteness and it showed on his face. Amelia chuckled. "You're just like your father, thinking women are only good for bearing children and doing house chores. My father wasn't a nobleman or gentry but he taught me a lot about business dealings. Do we know how much we've lost?"

"Mr. Maynard says it's quite a substantial amount and advised that I do all I can to find that ring before it is used to sell our house and other properties."

"This is big trouble," Amelia couldn't believe how foolish her sister-in-law had been. "That ring can cause us to lose everything. A person only has to produce a deed of sale with that seal to prove that they own the properties we have. Why did you trust your aunt with such a precious item?"

"Ma, I never thought she would actually take the ring. Her jewelery was hers to dispose of in any way, but she should never have touched the ring."

"Well, perhaps she felt that she was more of a Foxworth than you and I."

"Let'js not speak ill of the dead, Ma. The deed is done and now our priority is to find that ring and bring it back before we have more trouble."

"Very true! Blaming a person who isn't here is a waste of time. Do you have any idea who that Frenchman's accomplice could be?"

"In many cases it's usually a woman."

"You're being prejudiced."

"No Ma, just think. A scoundrel like Martineau could never trust another man. He most probably used another unsuspecting woman to carry out some of his crooked dealings."

Amelia nodded slowly. "You do have a point, but until we know the circles he moved in, we have no idea who this woman can be. She could be old, maybe his mother or young, a lover or mistress. The list is endless and I fear that by the time we catch up with the person, we'll have lost a lot."

"Please pray," Richard said in a soft, hoarse voice. He felt that he'd failed his mother and he couldn't imagine what would happen should they lose everything. Just a few months ago, head read about how the Lady Abigail Wentworth had trusted the same Frenchman and her family ended up losing everything. No one knew where the young lady was now and some suspected that she had committed suicide to escape the shame of that happening. In his case, his aunt had put his family in deep trouble and she wasn't here to see what happened. For a moment he felt angry at her but then compassion took over. How she must have suffered in her final days, knowing the grave mistake that she'd made.

"What are you thinking now?"

"About Aunt Edith."

Amelia scoffed. "Not that woman again!"

"Ma, I know you and my aunt never saw eye to eye, but please apply some compassion to your heart. Can you imagine how much suffering and torment she went through before her death? It's true she died of a broken heart knowing that she'd betrayed the family in the worst way possible. The torment and guilt must have ripped through her heart."

"Enough," Amelia held up a hand, feeling shaken. She'd never thought about her sister-in-law's state of mind in the days leading to her death. "Do all you can to find that ring, Richard. Your whole life and the future of this family depend on it."

"I'll do it, Ma."

Everything went well for Antoine, but only until she set foot in England. No one had questioned or bothered her on the coach between Paris and Calais and then on the ferry to Dover. In order to safeguard the ring she'd found, she wore it on her finger just in case her valise was stolen. Her priority was to get the ring back to the owners and she guarded it fiercely.

But the keen eyes of a customs officer spotted it and he pulled her over. "What's that you got over there?"

"Just my clothes," her heart was pounding.

"I mean on your finger."

"It's a family ring."

"Your family?"

"No sir. I'm returning it to the owners."

"Here, let me see it," he held out a hand and looked so fierce that Antoine had no choice than to pull it off her thumb because it was too big for her fingers. She handed it over to him and he observed it for a while then looked at her with piercing eyes. "Where did you find this ring?"

"Someone in Paris had it so I'm returning it to the family it belongs to."

"Young lady, I'm afraid you'll have to wait in holding for a while."

"Why? What have I done?"

"This ring belongs to the Duke of Hampshire's family and it's been missing for a year. That you have it in your possession makes you a suspect and they have to clear you before I can allow you out of here."

"Dear Lord," Antoine murmured under her breath. The man hadn't even glanced at her valise, what if he demanded that she open it and then he searched her clothes? But he didn't, being only interested in the ring, he put her in a small room. She had no idea how long she'd been locked up before two men who identified themselves as Bow Street Runners came and whisked her away.

Like the first customs officer, they had no interest in her valise but in the ring. "Young lady, you realize that you're in a lot of trouble, don't you?"

"I've done nothing wrong," she argued. "The ring was given to me by someone to deliver to the family to whom it belongs."

"And pray, what might this person's name be?"

"Does it matter?"

"Yes, for then we'll know whether you're guilty or not."

"Emile Martineau," she said at last and the men stared at her as if she'd just announced that she wanted to go and see the Regent. "He was my father."

"What's your name?"

"Antoinette Martineau," she said simply, knowing that she was putting herself into more trouble by associating with the man who was obviously well known by the two men.

"The duke himself will have to come and release you, for you need to explain how you got his family ring in the first place."

Richard was taking lunch with his mother when he received news that someone had been arrested and his family signet ring removed from them. The young lady was being held by Bow Street Runners in London for they'd arrested her just as she got off the ferry in Dover. He was glad he and his mother had decided to visit their town house in London and he didn't even bother finishing up his meal but was out like a shot. He hurriedly saddled his horse and took off.

"Wait for me," Amelia called out to no avail. She sighed and asked one of the servants to prepare a carriage for her. She also couldn't eat anything until she was sure the ring was back in safe custody.

Richard entered the precinct of the Bow Street Runners and identified himself even though most of the law enforcers knew him since he'd been frequenting the place in his search for the family heirloom. "Where is she?"

"Be patient, your grace. The ring is in our custody as is the young lady. We held her so you could question her."

"Thank you." Richard received the ring and clutched it in his palm, feeling very emotional all of a sudden. He couldn't believe that the ring had been found. "Thank you," he repeated. "May I see the young lady?"

"This way, your grace."

Antoine was seated on a hard chair and had laid her head on the small shaky table next to her when the door opened. She shot to her feet and when she saw the tall and distinguished looking man striding into the room, her heart sank. She'd imagined an elderly man to whom she would appeal for her freedom after explaining everything. This man didn't look like he would be easy to convince.

Richard saw the fleeting emotions on the young lady's face but closed his heart against any feelings of compassion. The young woman looked so innocent and frightened, but if she was an accomplice of the Frenchman, then she was well schooled on how to act innocent.

"What's your name, young lady?"

"Antoine. Antoine Martineau."

Richard recoiled as if he'd been struck. The woman was so beautiful and he'd hoped there was some explanation that would make him understand why she had his family ring.

Just hearing that dreadful name was enough to cause him to further harden his heart.

"The accomplice, no doubt," he said disdainfully and felt slightly guilty when he saw the flush on Antoine's face. "Are you any relation of that scoundrel, Emile Martineau?"

"He was my father," she said in a quiet voice, heart sinking. She would get no compassion from this man.

"You will pay for the crimes that you and that man committed."

"Richard!" He was so bent on questioning Antoine that he hadn't heard his mother come in behind him. "Listen to the poor woman first and then make your judgment."

"Mother, it's obvious this woman was Martineau's accomplice. Do you know that she's his daughter?"

"That doesn't give you the right to treat this poor woman badly until you listen to what she has to say." Amelia turned to Antoine. "Young lady, can you tell me how you came to be in possession of this ring?"

"Yes, ma'am."

"That's your grace to you," Richard said rudely, earning himself a glare from his mother. "She is the Duchess of Hampshire."

"Richard, I'll thank you to be silent for a while as I hear what Miss Martineau has to say."

"Thank you." Antoine felt that even though the duchess looked quite foreboding, there was a softer side to her. "My father was Emile Martineau but I've never seen him. I didn't even know whether he was dead or alive until a few weeks ago when his old trunk was delivered to me in Charente."

"Where's that?"

"Normandy. I've lived there all my life with my mother who passed away three years ago."

"I'm sorry for your loss."

"Among my father's things, I found a journal where my father had written about all the women he deceived and also where he had hidden the items he took from them. It took me some days to finally trace his hiding place but among those things I found this ring."

"You're such a little liar," Richard hissed. "You don't have any other items on your person and this ring is the only thing you were found with."

"Richard," but he ignored his mother.

"She's nothing more than a thief, mother. Why waste time on her."

"Silence," the duchess's voice was harsh and Richard shut up but sulked, glaring at Antoine. "Miss Martineau, you say you found something else?"

"Yes, mam," Antoine reached down and opened her valise and picked up one of her dresses. She ripped the hem and seam and put the items on the table. One by one, she tore her clothes and placed the items on the table until she was done. "In the journal which I have," she reached under her clothes and pulled out the journal. "My father indicated which particular item he took from whom. Some he sold to finance his wicked ventures, but everything else is there."

Richard couldn't believe his eyes and he could see that his mother was equally stunned.

"Please, I only want to return these things to the owners. Will you help me?"

"How do we know that you aren't deceiving us? All these items have to be authenticated that they aren't replicas and you have the real items."

"Very well then." Antoine felt really tired but relieved that she no longer was the custodian of the precious items.

4
SHOWING MERCY

Amelia was silent all the way home and her son got concerned. "Ma, what's wrong?"

"That poor girl," she said. "She took a great risk carrying all those precious gems from France to this place, and the best we could do was to have her locked up in jail. What kind of people are we, Richard?"

"Upright citizens, Ma. We don't know that she is telling the truth. What if she and her father sold the genuine things to throw everyone off track, he had her bring the fake ones here?"

"You heard the girl. She's never seen her father and her desire is to see that everything that was stolen is restored back to its owners."

"Do you believe such a cock and bull story, Ma?"

"Interestingly enough, it's too absurd to be a lie. I don't like what we've done."

"It's the right thing to do, mother. We have to find out the truth before feeling sorry for that woman."

"You really are a hypocrite, Richard. Your own aunt with her bare hands picked up her jewelery and the family ring and handed them over to a scoundrel, yet you showed her a lot of compassion. Yet here is this young woman, who took a great risk and brought back the stolen items and even more belonging to others, yet you treat her with so much disdain. She didn't have to. A wicked person would have taken it as an inheritance from her father and disappeared forever. Instead, Antoine Martineau has come all this way to make restitution and like the good English citizens that we are, we had her put in jail. It's just not right."

Richard knew that arguing with his mother would get him nowhere so he let it go. He would get to the bottom of the whole issue and see if the woman deserved to be cleared or judged.

For the next few days, Antoine was surprised when Amelia visited her in jail every single day. She brought her fresh food each time she came and even paid the jailer to get her out of the crowded cell into a private one. She also told Antoine about her sister-in-law and what her father had done to the poor woman, leading to her premature death.

"I'm really sorry you have to go through this," she told her. "My son insists on doing his investigations but the moment you're cleared, we will get you out of this place."

"Thank you, your grace."

"You really are a good child and all will be well."

Richard felt slightly ashamed when the investigators he sent brought him back the information that cleared Antoine of any wrong doing. The jeweler who was called in pronounced that all the articles that Antoine had brought were genuine and none had been replicated. He realized that he would have to eat humble pie and get the poor girl out of prison.

His mother would insist on making restitution and he sighed as he walked into the private cell.

"Miss Martineau, I come bearing good news." If he expected any sort of reaction from Antoine, he was disappointed. She fixed her blue eyes on him, giving him an unwavering stare that made him feel uncomfortable. She had a way of looking at a person that unnerved them, much like his mother. "Your name has been cleared and the items you brought are all genuine. We shall find a way of returning them to their owners."

Antoine merely shrugged. What did he expect her to say or do? She was innocent and knew it from the beginning so he really wasn't giving her any new information.

"I've come to take you home with me so that we can make up for the time you've spent in incarceration."

That was when she reacted. "The nerve," she said through clenched teeth. "You're the last person I would ever go anywhere with. After treating me like a common criminal you now come in here all apologetic and remorseful? No thank you, I will stay right here and if this is where my days on earth will end, so be it," and saying so, she turned her back on him.

Richard was stunned and speechless. He tried to plead with Antoine for he knew his mother wouldn't give him rest, but she didn't even turn around to look at him.

"Do you know that you're being disrespectful to me and I'm a duke."

"I'm already in prison, what more can they do to me? Hang me?"

"Don't say that. You're free to go and since you're a stranger in England, we would like to take care of you."

"I've already tasted of the hospitality of the English. Thank you for your kind offer but no thank you. When I leave here, I'll be on the first ferry back to France where I belong."

5

FREE AT LAST

It was Amelia who finally convinced Antoine to go home with them and she smiled when Richard practically fell over himself to make her comfortable. The journey from London to Hampshire was long and she was asleep for most of the way because she'd barely slept since setting foot in England.

She didn't know what to expect when she got to the family seat in Hampshire, but it definitely wasn't the royal treatment. Everyone made a fuss over her and she felt awed and humbled at the same time.

"You deserve all good things to come your way," Amelia told her. "You've had a very hard life through no fault of your own, and if there's anything I can do to make it easier from now on, all you have to do is ask."

"My greatest desire is to see that those gems, I brought back, are restored to their rightful owners, and also I would really like to trace my mother's family."

"Have you ever met any of them?"

"No, my lady. Mama left England nearly twenty years ago and never returned at all. She died three years ago without ever reconciling with her family. But she told me she was from a small town called Shepherds Cove in Lancashire. Her family name is Cummings and she told me it wasn't a very common name."

"My son will do all he can to find out whether your mother's family members are still alive and we'll help you to reunite with them."

"Thank you very much."

"May I ask a favour from you?"

"Yes, my lady."

"The French language has always fascinated me and over the years I tried to learn it. Will you teach me? Of course, I will pay you for your efforts."

"No, ma'am. I'm already enjoying so much of your hospitality and will be very happy to tutor you. That's the work I was doing back in Charente to earn my living. Mama taught me English and good French."

"You speak very good English, but can this be between us? I'd like people to think you're a long lost relative from

France who doesn't understand English. This will stop them from asking you all manner of questions for our neighbours and friends can be quite nosy."

"Ma, you'll frighten Miss Antoine into thinking we're a crazy lot of people."

"I don't want her harassed in any way, so please just don't mention anything to anyone and especially Beatrix."

Antoine saw Richard blushing and her interest was aroused, though she felt a slight pang within. She was being foolish and derided herself. Of course, a handsome duke like Richard Foxworth definitely had a woman in his life, apart from his mother.

"Why don't you want Beatrix to know that Antoine can understand English? Isn't that being devious?"

"Whenever that young lady visits her sister in France, she returns with great airs as if she's the first English woman to speak French."

"Ma, that's being unkind."

"But true, nevertheless."

Antoine was to find that Lady Amelia always spoke her mind, whether it made people uncomfortable or not. She longed to find out more about this Beatrix lady but didn't want to look like a nosy person so she held her peace.

She didn't have to wait for long, for that same evening, Lady Beatrix Manor presented herself to the house for dinner at Richard's invitation. Antoine was wearing one of Lady Amelia's old dresses for she had no wardrobe of her own. It was a beautiful silky jade gown that was slightly large for her. They'd not had time to make any adjustments but she felt warm inside when Richard couldn't seem to take his eyes off her.

But that was until Lady Beatrix floated into the room. She was a sensation and Antoine suddenly felt very dowdy in comparison. The fair lady clearly had her hooks into Richard for she dominated the conversation and wouldn't allow him to address her even for a single moment. Lady Amelia said nothing but observed all that was going on. When dinner was over, she immediately excused herself, leaving Antoine alone.

"Does this girl speak any English?" Antoine nearly smiled because Beatrix apparently believed that she didn't understand her language. "She looks really dowdy and unkempt. That's no way to appear at a duke's table. Didn't your mother tell her?"

"That's enough, Beatrix," Richard said. "It's not polite to talk about others as if they're not present. Miss Martineau is a guest in this house and should be treated with respect."

"Oh my love, please forgive me." Her tone was sickeningly sweet and Antoine wished she was anywhere but here. "I didn't mean any disrespect to your guest. I just wondered why she didn't dress better and yet I know how fussy you are when it comes to etiquette and formality."

"Mother will get her a new wardrobe tomorrow, so you won't have to worry about Miss Martineau's appearance."

6
HOSTILE NEIGHBOURS

B ut Beatrix was worried. She had seen Richard stealing glances at that French woman and didn't like what she saw. He was clearly besotted, and yet he was her man. From when they were teenagers, she'd marked Richard Foxworth as her territory and all the ladies in the immediate area and even beyond knew it.

Richard was a handsome man and his family had good money. He would make her a good husband and she'd been sure that he would propose very soon, but that was until the French woman arrived on the scene. Efforts to find out where she was from were futile and she tightened her lips as she paced her room.

"Something has to be done," she muttered, causing her personal maid to stop whatever she was doing.

"Did you say something, my lady?"

"Go back to your duties, Naomi and don't bother me again."

"I'm sorry, my lady."

Yes, she had to get rid of the usurper before her place was taken over. It would take careful planning but it had to be done in a hurry for she had a lot to lose.

Richard found himself smiling when he thought about Antoine. She was a feisty little thing and years of taking care of herself must have made her very tough. He liked that she didn't seem intimidated by his wealth or fawn over it. She treated him with respect, but not with awe.

If his mother read his thoughts, she would make him say penance prayers for she didn't like him behaving like a common lout as she would say.

Antoinette Martineau had saved his family's honour and he now had the ring safely in his bedroom drawer. The only person who entered his room was his personal valet and even Geoffrey knew better than to snoop among his things. He had a way of knowing when someone had been in his room and touched his things, so the servants were careful. In any case, they were very honest and had been with the family for a long time. They'd never had any incidences of theft even though the manor had very precious items.

Well, his aunt had taught him a great lesson and he would immediately take inventory of everything in the house and update the records. For one year he'd had his head in the clouds but not anymore. Aunt Edith might have sold more than she actually admitted and the only way he would know for sure was by meticulously going through the books his manager kept and physically checking the items off.

In the guest room, Antoine felt very restless and knew that it all had to do with the duke who was just a few doors away. She was really a simpleton to imagine that she could be in love with Richard Foxworth. What had happened to her convictions never to get involved with a man unless she knew him very well? She'd only known Richard for a few days but her heart had betrayed her.

7

THE KIDNAPPING

"I really need your help," Beatrix told Antoine and the latter looked at her blankly, like she couldn't understand what was being said. "I'm sorry, I'll ask Richard to translate what I'm saying." She was pulling her words like one would when talking to a child and Antoine really had to fight to keep her composure.

Richard was nowhere to be found and neither was his mother, so Beatrix tried all motions and in the end Antoine nodded as if she understood what was being said. This little game that the dowager duchess had started was amusing but it would have to stop at some point. She couldn't go on pretending that she didn't understand English, and she always had to be careful while she was around Beatrix or the servants. It was exhausting, to say the least.

"My carriage is coming to get us, and will take us to my home so you can help me with some embroidery."

The carriage came but Antoine was surprised when Beatrix didn't board it, but bid the two men in it to drive it away once she had climbed in. They laughed wickedly and Antoine knew she was in trouble. She couldn't believe that she'd been fooled so easily, that was the trouble with being overconfident, she thought.

"The lady directed us to take this one away and keep her for as long as we want," the younger of the two men said in a voice that made Antoine go cold all over. "Foolish broad doesn't understand a single word of English."

"We're not to harm her in any way," the second man said. "Or we shall be hanged and I don't intend for that to happen. The lady said we're to hold her for a day or two and then release her. By then the young duke will have lost all interest for he will believe that she's spoiled goods. But we're not to touch her at all, unless you want your head served to you on a platter."

The first man grumbled but fell silent when the second glared at him. Antoine knew that the best thing for her to do would be to feign innocence all through and act like she had no idea that she was being kidnapped. That would cause the men to lower their guard and at the first chance she got, she would flee.

"Look at her, so innocent and foolish and yet a trap is being set for her."

"Do you think the lady will get away with it?"

"She's shrewd and the plan will work. Hiding the signet ring and jewelery and telling the duke that this one has fled with them isn't difficult. Once he swallows the bait, we shall release her and she won't be able to defend herself for the items won't be found. The best place for her will be jail, for the lady said the duke would never forgive her for taking the family ring."

"I just hope the pay is worth it."

"It will be."

The carriage came to a stop outside a small cottage and Antoine raised a curious face to the two men. "Where?" She had to pretend to at least speak a word or two of English. "Where my lady?"

The two men guffawed at her efforts and motioned for her to climb down from the carriage. Even as she climbed down, her eyes were already searching for an escape route. They hadn't traveled too far from the manor and she was sure she could find her way home even in the dark.

8

THE SEARCH

"Ma, do you think Antoine would do such a heinous thing as Beatrix is claiming?"

"That young girl may have been here for only a few days but she's as honest as day. I wouldn't be in a hurry to believe whatever I'm told, especially by Beatrix."

"Ma, why do you say that?"

"Because from the moment she set eyes on Antoine, she has wanted to get rid of her. I just pray she hasn't harmed the girl in any way."

"But what if Antoine has truly run away?" Richard felt as though his heart was breaking. He loved Antoine and had been thinking of a way to express his feelings to her when Beatrix arrived at the house and told him that she'd seen

Antoine in the company of two men who seemed like shady characters.

"You can never trust these French," she'd said. "Make sure that there's nothing missing from the house. You've given that strange woman too much freedom in this house. Why, the other day I found her in your mother's bedroom as I was on my way to find the duchess."

"What was she doing there?" Richard frowned, not wanting to believe what he was hearing.

"She was going through your mother's drawers and when she saw me, she was shocked. Though she said nothing and tried to pretend that she was lost, the guilt was written all over her face."

And truly when Richard checked his drawers, he found that the family ring was missing and his mother also said some of her jewelery was gone too. He was angry at first and nearly believed what Beatrix had told him but then paused for a while. Why would Antoine bring him the ring all the way from Paris and then steal it once again? It just didn't make sense and instead of getting the village constable to come and investigate like Beatrix demanded, he decided to carry out his own investigation.

"I don't trust Beatrix but since nobody saw her leaving with Antoine, I'll give her the benefit of the doubt," Amelia said. "I pray that the girl is alright."

"Me too, mother," Richard was clearly upset and his state of discomfort made his mother smile inwardly. She'd come to love Antoine and knew that the young lady would make a good wife for her son. That he was disturbed meant that he had feelings for her, and he was also willing to give her a chance to redeem herself.

"Antoine will come home, she must come home where it is safe," Amelia said, praying that the girl was alright.

9

ESCAPING FROM THE CAPTORS

The two men snored like sows and Antoine wondered what kind of guards they were supposed to be. She couldn't sleep because she didn't trust the younger man not to attack her as the older one slept.

They'd pushed her into the second room of the cottage and kept the door shut but not locked and she kept expecting one of them, mostly the younger one to walk in and begin harassing her. She wasn't even offered supper though she heard them eating and her stomach growled in protest. The last meal she'd had was a mid morning snack with the duchess.

What was Richard thinking about her right now? Would he believe Beatrix when she told him that Antoine had stolen his ring and some of his mother's jewelery? Would the duchess defend her in the light of these new allegations?

What had she ever done to Beatrix to merit such unkindness, she wondered. If it was all about the duke, he barely acknowledged her unless his mother was present. The two of them suited each other with their snobbish ways, but a small voice within her protested. Richard was no snob, he was just brought up differently from her. But would he bother looking for her or would he believe that she had run away with his property?

She couldn't stay here and wait for trouble to come to her. Escaping through the door was out of the question for she might wake the men up, so she turned her attention to the bolted window. Touching one of the boards, she nearly cried out in joy when it came apart in her hand. This was an old wood cutter's cottage and in a state of disrepair. The two men probably thought she was one of those delicate women who couldn't take care of herself.

The window creaked and she quickly left it alone, for fear of waking the sleeping men. She waited for a short while but when no one came, gathered her courage once again and pushed the window wider and scrambled out. Those wild adventures with her charges back in Charente were paying off. The three boys, now young men had taught her how to climb trees, jump over fences and even ride without a saddle. She crouched beneath the window and waited to hear a shout but nothing happened once again and she crept along the wall until she reached where the two horses had been tethered.

Thank goodness for her life in the French countryside for she could ride very well and was soon on her way. She got lost a couple of times before finding the road that led to the house. Stopping the horse a distance away, she got down and went the rest of the way on foot, leading the horse. He was a gentle gelding and she tethered him to a tree then used the kitchen door, which she found open. Her first stop was the duchess's room.

Amelia thought she was dreaming when she saw Antoine standing before her. "What happened to you, child?"

"I got kidnapped by two men but managed to escape. They believed that I couldn't understand English so they spoke of their plans."

"I don't understand how you could get into a carriage with people you don't know. Don't you know that you could have been badly harmed?"

"It was Beatrix who made me believe that she needed my help with some embroidery and we were going to her home. When I got into the carriage, she immediately dismissed it."

"I wonder how none of our servants saw what was happening."

"They must have thought that it was normal for I didn't seem to be under any kind of restraint or stress. I walked to the carriage myself and got in so they didn't think that anything was wrong."

"Where are these men that took you? Do you think you can lead the constable to them?"

"Yes, ma'am."

"Wait here then, let me get Richard and tell him what has happened."

Richard listened to Antoine and when she was done, did a surprising thing. Right before his mother, he pulled her into his arms. "I'm glad you weren't harmed in any way, for tomorrow people would have been hanged. I had determined that I was going to force Beatrix to tell me what she knew."

"Richard, we're wasting time and it will soon be morning. If those men wake up and find Antoine gone, they will know she has escaped and she'll never be safe. Get some men and go and arrest them right now."

"A good thing my two friends who are Bow Street Runners are at the village inn. A few days ago, I asked them to come to Hampshire so they could help trace Antoine's mother's family. I was waiting for morning to also ask them to help me search for her."

"Our servants are trustworthy so send one of them to get those law officers as Antoine shows you where she was held. When the Bow Street Runners get to that cottage, bring Antoine back here yourself."

"I'm never letting her out of my sight again, Mother. You can be sure of that. But we have to keep her hidden for a while so I can set a trap for Beatrix. I want to see what she'll tell me tomorrow."

"This has been a very unfortunate incident which might have turned out very badly but for Antoine's bravery." The duchess hugged Antoine. "I'm glad you're safe, dear girl."

Capturing the two kidnappers was easy, but getting Beatrix to incriminate herself would be something else. Richard decided that he wouldn't reveal that the men had been arrested until he had made her spill out what she knew.

So the men were held in one of the back rooms, bound and gagged and under the watchful eye of the two Bow Street Runners.

The next morning, Beatrix came in just as the village constable was also coming in. "It's a good thing you're here, sir," she told him. "There's been trouble and I kept asking Richard to send for you but he was hesitant."

"What seems to be the problem, my lady?"

"There's a French woman who was staying here. She stole Richard's ring and Lady Amelia's jewelery and ran away. You have to find her and see that she pays for her crimes. You can never trust strangers."

"Is that right, your grace?" the constable turned to Richard.

"Indeed it is as Lady Beatrix reports," he said evasively.

"Do I detect a note of doubt in your voice, your grace?"

"I'd just like for Lady Beatrix to tell you where she was when she saw Antoine running away."

Beatrix frowned, looking sharply at Richard. "Are you doubting my word now, your grace?"

"No, my lady, but in the time since you reported her missing, I got contrary news to what you told me yesterday."

Beatrix looked uncomfortable and Richard wanted to smile but kept a straight face. "Even the duchess confirmed that her jewelery is missing."

"Mama told me that there were some pieces that she'd taken to the goldsmith for adjusting."

"I'm sure some others are missing from her drawer," Beatrix insisted and when she glanced at Richard and saw the strange look on his face, she knew that her secret was out. But how, she'd been very careful and paid the two men some good money. They owed her and couldn't betray her. She had to get out of here and find out what was going on.

But before she could rise up, the door opened and her two accomplices were pushed into the room. Beatrix turned as white as a sheet and Amelia thought she was about to swoon.

"What's the matter, my lady?" The constable was clearly the only one who didn't know what was going on. "Would you like a glass of water?"

"Please," she said in a hoarse voice, looking anywhere but at the men.

Richard took over. "Who are you and what are you doing here?" He demanded of the two men. They were properly cowered and the older one pointed at Beatrix.

"Your grace," his voice trembled. "That is the lady who told us to take the French woman away from here. We didn't intend to harm the lady in any way but were only holding her for a day or two. We would have released her unharmed. Upon my soul, your grace, we didn't touch a single hair on her head."

"The fact that you took Miss Martineau away from here against her will is tantamount to harming her. You will hang for your crimes."

"Mercy, your grace," the younger man cried out. "We intended no harm but were enticed with money. The lady said she had taken your family ring and your mother's jewelery so you would think it was the French lady who did it."

"You lie," Beatrix screamed but Richard only raised an eyebrow. She rushed to his side and clutched his arm.

"Please say that you believe me, my love. I would never do anything sinister like that. It must be that woman who put these men up to it and she's no doubt laughing behind all our backs as she returns to France."

Richard's response was turn. "Antoine, please do come out here."

For the second time that early morning, Beatrix turned quite pale.

Antoine stepped out from behind the closed door and Richard held out his hand. She walked to him without any hesitation. He pulled her close and she nearly stopped breathing. What was going on?

"Constable, this woman clearly intended to harm my beloved."

"Your beloved?" Both women looked at him in astonishment.

"Yes," he kissed Antoine's forehead. "You are my beloved," he turned to Beatrix. "This French woman speaks fluent English and you've been caught in your own lie. Now, before this gets out of hand, may I have the ring that you stole as well as my mother's jewelery?"

Beatrix tried to deny it but when she realized that she was cornered, indicated one of the large vases in the living room. "I dropped them in there and would have returned them."

"That was very unkind of you," Amelia's tone and look were disapproving. "I don't ever want to see you in my house again." She rang the bell for a servant who she instructed and a few minutes later, he returned with all the missing items.

"You intended to harm an innocent woman and all for what? Because you believe yourself to be in love with me?"

"But I love you, Richard."

"Beatrix," he spoke patiently as one would to a child. "We've been through this before and I told you that I love you as a sister, never as a wife or lover. You're beautiful and can make a good match with someone else but not me. What possessed you to do something so terrible and think you could get away with it?"

"I'm sorry, but I love you so much and didn't think. Please forgive me."

"I forgive you but on one condition."

"Anything, Richard."

"What you've done could cause you to be shunned by society but I won't subject you to such humiliation. Instead, these two friends of mine and the constable will escort you and these two men to London. These men will face serious charges and you will be taken to Dover to catch the ferry to France. I'm sure your sister will be happy to receive you and make sure that you never set foot in England again, not while I live. For if you do that, I will prosecute you for there are enough witnesses here for you to be charged with a very serious crime. Kidnapping someone and planting false evidence against them is punishable by a long term in jail or hanging."

"Please no, I won't repeat it again," Beatrix was weeping.

"You're not to be trusted and for as long as you're still here, my love will never be safe."

Antoine thought she would fly because her heart soared. Richard loved her, else he wouldn't have called her his love. Was this what it felt like to be in love, she wondered. It was as if everything was bright and shone that morning.

The three partners in crime were taken away. Amelia come over to Antoine. "I'm so happy that you're safe," she hugged her.

"Thank you, my lady."

"Don't you think you should start getting used to calling me Mother, seeing as you're soon going to be my son's wife?"

"He hasn't asked me yet," Antoine retorted good naturedly.

"Then he better do so or my patience will soon run out. Don't you think it's about time that he settled down?"

"It's as you say, my lady."

"I'm right here," Richard protested, a huge smile on his face. He took Antoine's face between his hands. "We've really treated you badly since you set foot in this country and I want to say how sorry we are, my darling."

"All's well," Antoine murmured.

"You know that I fell in love with you the very first time I set my eyes on you, but I was so disappointed because I thought you were Mr. Martineau's accomplice. Still, I couldn't get you out of my head and one of the reasons I kept you in prison was so you wouldn't return to France before I had found out what was going on."

"Please forgive us, my dear."

"Mother, there's nothing to forgive."

"The women in my life talk too much," Richard glared at the two of them. "This day shouldn't go on before you give me an answer. I can see that Antoine is really exhausted from all the excitement and I'd like for her to rest. But not before I get the answer I seek."

"You haven't asked me a question," Antoine said cheekily. Amelia knew she had found the perfect woman for her son. This was just the woman to keep Richard on his toes but also who loved him genuinely.

A growl came from Richard's throat, earning him a fierce look from his mother. "Really Richard, growling like a bear?"

"I'm sorry Ma, but please let me complete what I have begun."

"Go ahead"

He nodded in satisfaction on getting his mother's approval. "Antoine, I love you so much and want you to be my duchess. I promise to take care of you for the rest of my life. Will you marry me, my darling?"

"Try and stop me."

"What kind of answer is that?"

"Richard, take it any way it's given to you. At least, I didn't hear her say no."

"Mother, let me just put him out of his misery." She raised herself on tiptoe and kissed his cheek. "Your grace, it will be an honour to be your wife."

"Why?"

"Because I love you and you're the one man that I can't live without."

And Amelia clapped her hands cheerfully.

10

EPILOGUE – MAKING RESTITUTION

All the jewelery that Antoine had brought from her father's vault was eventually returned to the owners, who couldn't believe it. They tried to offer her rewards but she wouldn't take anything. "My father wronged you and for that I beg for your forgiveness. Please forgive him for he is facing his judgment." Because she was so contrite, all those she spoke too immediately said they had forgiven the ills done to them.

Antoine left the house one afternoon when Richard was in his study with the estate manager and his mother was sleeping. She walked to the family burial ground and stood before Edith Foxworth's grave. "I know that it's too late and you lost your life because of my father," she shook her head sadly. "I'm so sorry for the pain you must have gone through and just wish you were here so I could tell all this to your face. Please forgive us Lord, don't count this sin against me and my descendants to come."

Perhaps the most joyous occasion was when Lord and Lady Richard Foxworth as well as the Dowager Duchess made their way to Somerset to see Lady Abigail Birch, the Duchess of Dorchester and returned her stolen jewelery.

She wept in her husband's arms as she thanked them for their kindness.

One thing put a blight on an otherwise joyous season for Lady Antoine Foxworth. The fact that the Bow Street Runners who were charged with finding her mother's relatives brought back a sad report.

"The only Cummings alive are distant relatives and not by blood but by marriage. I'm sorry, your grace, Lady Antoine's relatives are long dead."

And it was her turn to weep for the relatives she would never know and her mother's broken life and dreams.

The wise duke let his duchess cry her grief out and soon she was smiling once again and it seemed as if the sun had come out from behind a cloud.

"I will never know my family but I have found a new family now," she kissed her husband and hugged her mother-in-law. "This is the time for me to begin a new generation."

"And we're honoured to be a part of it," Lady Amelia the dowager said.

"My beloved wife, you'll never be alone again."

"Thank you for loving me, Richard."

"And you for loving me, Antoine."

THANK YOU FOR CHOOSING A PUREREAD BOOK!

We hope you enjoyed the story, and as a way to thank you for choosing PureRead we'd like to send you this free book, and other fun reader rewards...

An undercover plan designed to win a young nobleman's heart is threatened when the lovely Gabrielle Belgrade's soft conscience and honesty threatens to undo the matchmaking shenanigans of Lord Grant's well intentioned godmother.

Click here for your free copy of The Pretender
PureRead.com/regency

Thanks again for reading.
See you soon!

LOVE CLEAN & WHOLESOME REGENCY ROMANCE?

DIVE INTO THESE DELIGHTFUL BOXSETS...

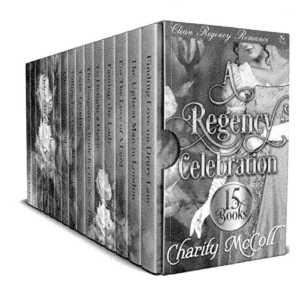

Read Regency Celebration On Amazon

Read PureRead Regency Romance On Amazon

Read Seasons of Regency Romance on Amazon

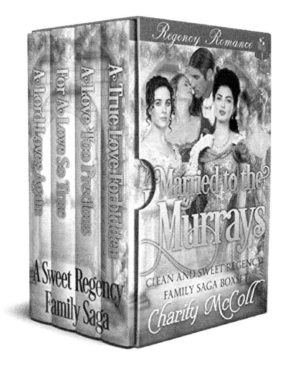

Read Married To The Murrays

OUR GIFT TO YOU

AS A WAY TO SAY THANK YOU WE WOULD LOVE TO SEND YOU THIS BEAUTIFUL STORY FREE OF CHARGE.

An undercover plan designed to win a young nobleman's heart is threatened when the lovely Gabrielle Belgrade's soft conscience and honesty threatens to undo the matchmaking shenanigans of Lord Grant's well intentioned godmother.

Click here for your free copy of The Pretender

PureRead.com/regency

At PureRead we publish books you can trust. Great tales without smut or swearing, but with all of the mystery and romance you expect from a great story.

Be the first to know when we release new books, take part in our fun competitions, and get surprise free books in your inbox by signing up to our free VIP Reader list.

As a thank you you'll receive a copy of **The Pretender** straight away in you inbox.

Click here for your free copy of The Pretender

PureRead.com/regency

Printed in Great Britain
by Amazon

24612544R00115